THE THREE EXTRAS

John Rullo

GSP
GIANT STEPS PRESS

Advance Praise for The Three Extras

The Three Extras is a bittersweet coming of age fantasy spanning the lifelong friendship of three fellows whose paths were destined to meet and ultimately lead them to greatness. John Rullo has once again penned a tale that baby boomers will embrace, bringing smiles to their faces, tears to their eyes and hope to their futures. Never give up; you don't know when that ship is coming in!

~~~Eric Foley, *American Avatar*

Funny, poignant, and sometimes even erotic, author John Rullo takes the reader on a tender trip through time, recounting the notable events in the lifelong friendship of three high school classmates. He has created a heart-rending tale of camaraderie and mortality by tracing their lives from reckless youth through the trials and tribulations of growing old. Combined with a comedic peek into Hollywood, *The Three Extras* is a thoroughly entertaining read!

~~~ R. Gavarian, *Gold Coast Review*

The Three Extras had to be written with the big screen in mind! With every chapter, I couldn't help but imagine what a captivating film John Rullo's wonderful story would make; a fun-filled adventure driving home the point that life is definitely too short. Embrace every moment!

~~~Robert Woods

John Rullo has treated us with a joyfully nostalgic look into the 60's and 70's and magically weaved it into a playful stab at modern day Hollywood through the lives of three very likable characters. *The Three Extras* is a funny, sad, and sometimes sexy tale that celebrates friendship and life in all of its stages. You won't want it to end!

~~~G. Talia, *Health and Yoga News*

Copyright © 2013 Giant Steps Press

All rights reserved. No part of this publication may be reproduced or transmitted in any form or by any means, electronic or mechanical, including photocopy, recording, or any information storage and retrieval system, without permission in writing from the publisher, except for brief quotes in reviews.

ISBN-13: 978-1484149317

ISBN-10: 1484149319

Cover design by: J T Millstead
Book Design: Norman Ball
Back cover photo by: Gerard Comito

Giant Steps Press
Freeport, NY 11520
www.giantstepspress.com

Many thanks go out to Jack, Wiley, Toni-Ann, and Gina for their lifelong friendship; I don't know how I would have survived without you…

~

Carolyn, thanks for the encouragement and the extra pair of eyes

~

Thanks to Joann for a lifetime of love and contending with my big dreams and many eccentricities!

~

Table of Contents

I ~DESTINY CALLS~

II ~DEATH, WHERE IS THY STING?~

III ~THE DIRTY DISCIPLES~

IV ~ELECTRIC DUST~

V ~EVERYTHING CHANGES~

VI ~INTERMISSION~

VII ~WHEN DID THIS HAPPEN?~

VIII ~SEEING STARS~

IX ~IT COMES WITH THE TERRITORY~

X ~ALMOST RICH, BARELY FAMOUS~

XI ~WARNING SIGN~

XII ~WHEN YOU LEAST EXPECT IT~

XIII ~DIDN'T WE JUST DO THIS?~

XIV ~IT WAS NICE WHILE IT LASTED~

XV ~THE END OF THE LINE~

XVI ~FAREWELL~

THE THREE EXTRAS

John Rullo

~DESTINY CALLS~

~From the moment my eyes thoroughly studied Willy Taylor and Jack Reilly when they came wandering into Home Room 107 ten minutes late on the first day of class, something told me I had found my lifelines and that an everlasting friendship was about to begin. There was something defiant in their stance, something rebellious in their appearance. For some reason, their aura brought to mind why I so admired the likes of Marlon Brando and James Dean: nonconformists who refused to take shit from anyone. I could definitely relate. From the depths of my sleepy soul, a strange and unfamiliar feeling had been stirring, filling me with the joyful awareness that I wasn't like everybody else. I yearned to be true to my rebellious spirit, yet I was uncertain if I had what it took to stand alone like my silver screen idols.

How and why Jack, Willy and I happened to voluntarily end up in a strict, all-boy Catholic High School, such as St. Stanislaw's, was no mystery. That was just the norm, the natural progression for kids like us from suburban Roman Catholic families: Baptism, Confirmation, and Holy Communion along with twelve years of schooling under the heavenly tutelage of the highly revered staff of sexually repressed men and women of the cloth. When we were in grade school, our unsuspecting parents straightened our plaid navy blue ties, packed our Lone Ranger lunch boxes with nitrate-enriched deli meat on Wonder Bread sandwiches, and sent us on our way with no idea of the scandalous intentions of the priests who were on hand to absolve us of our nasty little sins. They just followed in the footsteps of the comfortably dumb generations before them, never considering that someday some of us would awaken. I remember receiving the *St. Stanislaw Rule Book* in the mail shortly after making my decision to attend and I thought, "Maybe I made a big mistake; James Dean would never allow himself to be in this situation!" The dress code alone was enough to scare away anyone, especially an aspiring young rock and roll star like me. As it turned out, it wasn't a mistake. It was destiny.

Jack and Willy handed Brother Richard their tardy slips, then made their way to the back of the classroom where they took seats on either side of me. Both of them looked as if they took some serious efforts in lacquering their hair as to make it appear regulation. Jack's thick, long, jet-black strands were combed straight back forming a dense "V" just above his muddy-white shirt collar. His fair white skin, sculpted jaw and streamlined nose proudly announced his deep-rooted Irish heritage. There was no denying Jack was ever going to have any trouble attracting girls; to say he was one good looking lad would be a huge understatement. The contrast in our appearance made his being Irish as unmistakable as my olive complexion and slightly extended nose made me Italian. Willy seemed to visibly bridge the difference between Jack and me, so it was hard to tell what part of the world his ancestors hailed from. Slightly darker than Jack and slightly lighter than me, I later learned that Willy's roots were many. Parts Italian, Irish, German, Swedish, Norwegian and American Indian, he was indeed a true mutt. His well-defined chin and sloping nose made him interestingly handsome. His eyes were a unique shade of green, seeming to shift from dark forest to light ocean depending on the intensity of the surrounding light. Willy never slouched.

His perfect posture demanded one's attention, yet he rarely had too much to say; a gentle soul, non-confrontational, yet committed and cool. In my imagination his profile brought to mind a French painter. I could almost see a black beret perched upon his head as he painstakingly brushed the finishing touches to his latest portrait. In reality, however, his wild, bushy mane was pulled back as tightly as possible, pasted in place, giving the impression there was a bee hive protruding from the back of his skull. The trick was to not let the hair hang over the collar, which was why the three of us always appeared to be walking about with our necks stretched as much as we could, and our faces always positioned downward. I had trimmed my hair considerably a week before the start of the school year, but even after my half-hearted attempt at conforming, I could not risk foregoing what would become my morning ritual of fastening my unruly locks securely in place with whatever hair goops and sprays my mom had in the bathroom cabinets. For the four years we remained in St. Stanislaw's, that was the cautionary procedure the three of us followed every weekday, just so we could look as cool as we imagined ourselves to be when we "let our freak flags fly" outside the confines of high school. Without their trusted companionship, I wouldn't have lasted a week.

We were three outcasts sitting among the thirty-six geeky male teenage classmates all who sported fresh conventional haircuts, penny loafers, brand new Robert Hall sports jackets and uninspiring banker's ties, complete with the tightly pulled asphyxiating Windsor knot. Although Jack, Willy and I also donned the required jacket and tie, we worked hard at not looking like everybody else. Jack and Willy wore thin, solid black, British rock band style ties and knotted them loosely in the simpler "four-in-hand" method. Until a Brother told them to button it, they usually kept the top button of their shirts rebelliously unbuttoned. Jack dressed in the same greenish-brown sport jacket every day, and although it always looked as if he kept it rolled up in a ball when he wasn't wearing it, it was way cool, appearing, from a distance, somewhat like a well-worn army jacket. Willy was more of the clothes horse. Among his collection of Mod sports jackets was the one he wore most often, the light gray with the collar outlined in black velvet, like The Beatles wore on Ed Sullivan. I wasn't as particular about my jackets, but as long as my pants were tight, my shoes were pointed, and my ties were loud psychedelic colors, I felt secure in my coolness. Sometimes I think we enjoyed the challenge of seeing just how far we could push the limits of the school dress code and sometimes I think we simply craved the attention. Growing up in households that were just starting to show cracks in their conservative shells, each of our parents hesitantly supported our passion to be individuals by permitting us to challenge the Catholic school establishment. By choosing their battles they had hoped their leniency would keep us walking the straight and narrow in a world they sensed was in for big changes.

John Rullo

~DEATH, WHERE IS THY STING? ~

Staring down into Jack's open casket, it was hard for Willy and me to believe those days of ducking in and out of boys' rooms and stairwells to avoid detention for breaking the dress code was over seventy-five years ago. Who'd have ever thought his lavish locks of glossy black hair would one day shed, only to be replaced with the trademark Yankee cap which he never removed from his head, not even in death?

While he was in his mid-seventies, Jack's health started failing terribly, which is the reason we had stopped appearing in movies. We made a pact right around the time our career had just started to skyrocket; we vowed, "Either we remain in this together, or we don't remain in it at all!" No different than it was in high school, none of us would have survived without the others. Jack was the one who lit the fire under our asses; he pushed. He loved Hollywood, living in California, and especially seeing us together on the big screen. He just never seemed to tire of it. Willy and I, on the other hand, were content to be living in West Palm Beach, Florida, in the neighboring homes we dreamed about owning before we became successful as screen stars later in our lives. We owed it all to Jack, so whenever we got the call informing us that our services were needed, we just packed our bags and booked our flights because we never wanted to disappoint him. Life is funny. Opportunity, just like death, comes knocking when it's least expected.

The Three Extras

The wake was held in Floral Park, New York, the town Jack lived in before his lifelong dream of moving to California became a reality. His children and grandchildren were all still living in the vicinity, so they made the decision to have his body shipped back to the east coast. Unlike Willy and me, who had lost our spouses within the same year, Jack's high school sweetheart, Jennifer, who remained his wife for 65 years, was still very much alive. Jenny, surrounded by their seven grandchildren, was standing in front of the coffin when Willy and I first entered the room. One of the kids, although they were now adults, alerted her to our arrival. As she slowly turned, from behind the glasses that sat so elegantly upon her slender nose I could see the gleam in her tired eyes. With the help of her handsome grandson, Jenny carefully squeezed through the crowd making her way over to greet us.

"How the fuck did this happen, John Colletti?" she asked as she reached her arms outward for a hug. For as long as I've known Jenny, she has always affectionately addressed all of her friends and loved ones with both first and last names.

"How did what happen, Jenny Reilly?" I replied, not knowing if she was referring to her husband's passing away or something more.

"How did we get so fuckin' old?" she snapped, followed by her all too familiar curt laugh.

"You must have read my mind, Jenny. I was just thinking about when we all met. I'm gonna miss him."

As I answered her, Willy nudged me, and being the realist he's always been, reminded me that it may not be too far in the future that each of us was going to be laid out in our very own pine box.

I guess everything is relative, but Jenny looked and sounded pretty good for a woman in her mid-eighties. She was still quick-witted and her eyes maintained their ability to penetrate. No one could ever lie to Jenny without her knowing it; she could see right through them. More than anything, she hated being lied to. In fact, the one and only time Jack was in a compromising position of any kind, she absolutely knew. The three of us thought we had concocted the perfect lie, complete with alibis, whereabouts, and time frames, but she cut right through our story like a chainsaw, bringing Jack to his knees with a confession, tears and an apology, leaving Willy and me looking like two idiotic traitors, even though, theoretically, he did nothing wrong! I always assumed she considered our embarrassment and the guilt of our betrayal penance enough, because she forgave us almost immediately and never brought up the incident again. In defense of Jack, the seductress was a beautiful young starlet we met on a set who just so happened to have had a Jack fixation. Her mind was obviously set on doing whatever necessary to have her way with him, but as we learned, even the best laid plans can go awry. I always secretly wished it was me she desired, but Willy and I had our own memorable adventures that we had managed to keep to ourselves through the years.

The funeral parlor was overflowing with faces, both familiar and unfamiliar. To see such a large turnout of friends, fans, family, and industry people, many who came from out of town, was quite the tribute to our deceased partner. Jack and Jenny had two sons and a daughter, all in their fifties, who did an outstanding job of seeing to it that their father's wake was a joyful celebration of his life and his achievements rather than the standard solemn, boring, depressing, obligatory gathering. In lieu of flowers, the family had requested that donations be made to the various charities the Reilly's gave to so generously over the years. Truth be told, the room was so decked out with movie memorabilia, there was no room for flowers. There were posters, photographs, and life-size cardboard cutouts of me, Jack, and Willy on display in every square inch of the funeral home. Having been away from the scene for a few years, I was beginning to feel a little bit self-conscious seeing my face wherever I glanced. Willy, on the other hand, kept proudly pointing them out to me. "Hey, Johnny," he called out, "Remember when we shot this one? We had so much fun on that set!"

This was undoubtedly one of the most interesting wakes I'd ever attended, and at this time in my life, I'd been to plenty. Waitresses, dressed in old-fashioned movie theatre matron uniforms, were milling about the chatty crowd with trays of hors d'oeuvres, while bartenders manned the several rolling bars pouring champagne and assorted shots. Every so often, someone would raise his glass and shout, "Here's to The Three Extras." Willy and I would acknowledge him with a nod and then toast to our buddy. It was like old home week being back in New York seeing family, friends and so many of the people we'd worked with through the years. For a moment it seemed as though Willy and I were out of retirement, back in the limelight, getting so much attention from all those who supposedly came to pay their respects. Suddenly, however, the allure of being celebrities got squashed like a squirrel under the tires of a 4X4 when we remembered our vow, "We're all in this together, or we're not in it at all." It was always the three of us or nothing; that's the way we said it was going to be, and that's the way it stayed. Without Jack standing alongside us, we were just average guys; an Abbott without a Costello or a Laurel without a Hardy. At that sobering second, Willy tugged on my sleeve and whispered, "Hey Johnny, isn't that Veronica Pond?" pointing inconspicuously to an attractive blond who just gracefully entered the room. I couldn't believe my eyes. It was definitely Veronica posing behind those white-framed sunglasses and she looked remarkable. I don't think I'll ever forget her. The only moment I was ever jealous of Jack was when Veronica almost succeeded in seducing him in our trailer. It was the only time in our career when a woman was able to totally captivate Jack. We knew if we had ever left them alone together, Delilah would have had her way with our Samson. I'll never forget the evening Veronica gave us the eye and pointed to the door without ever letting Jack out of her sight. We'd immediately gotten the hint. Quickly doing the math in my head, I figured she had to be closing in on 70. She was still quite eye-catching in her old age. She spotted us.

"Hey boys!" she called out softly in that still-familiar sultry voice, "It's been a while, hasn't it?"

"Veronica!" we called out in unison, "You look fabulous!"

"You two aren't looking so bad yourselves with those sexy tans!" she said, returning the compliment.

Without missing a beat, Jenny made her way over and joined the conversation. "John Colletti and Willy Taylor, are you guys going to introduce me to your friend or not?"

"I guess it's about time you two meet," Willy complied, "Jenny, this is Veronica Pond; Veronica, meet Jenny Reilly."

"Oh!" Veronica cried, "You must be Jack's wife! He always spoke so highly of you."

"When?" Jenny snapped, "When you were fucking him? What do you think; I don't know who you are?"

"Jenny!" I cut in like a referee in a boxing ring, "That happened years ago, let it go for Christ's sake!"

The Three Extras

"Relax, John Colletti," Jenny laughed, "I'm just screwing with her!"

From where I stood, it was quite the ironic scene to see the peak of Jack's Yankee cap protruding from the coffin in the background, while in the foreground Jenny, turning to Veronica, reached out her hand and said, "Nice to finally meet you Veronica Pond, nice to finally meet you!"

That was the Jennifer I knew and loved; never could tell at first if she was putting someone on or not. Willy and I mingled about as Jenny and Veronica carried on like giggling schoolgirls sharing powder room gossip.

Although I envisioned myself as the virile 56 year old I was when I first appeared on a movie set, the hard reality was that in just a few months I was going to be 85 years old. The champagne and the bourbon shots were getting to me and I was extremely exhausted from the combination of traveling and kissing, hugging and shaking hands with people for the entire evening. I was getting too old for small talk, sex, and I especially didn't need to make any more connections or friends. Willy and I were happy living the last chapter of our lives in our quiet Florida beach community where we got regular visits from our kids and our grandkids. We read books, strummed our guitars, waded in the ocean, ate at our favorite restaurants and reminisced about the crazy events of our lives. We were fortunate to be alive and in relatively good health. Unlike Jack and many of our colleagues, we managed to escape the use of canes and walkers. We dodged knee replacements, heart attacks, prostate cancer, dementia and baldness! We made more money than we ever dreamed possible, so in many ways, we were blessed.

The viewing went on way past closing time, but that was certainly to be expected. Jack was popular and well-liked in the community even before show business entered his life. After managing his sons' Little League team for a few years, he became Floral Park's Commissioner of Baseball. His radiant personality and good looks had initiated a movement to have him run for town mayor, an offer he'd politely turn down.

Willy and I knew we had another long and exhausting day ahead of us. Although Jack hasn't been a practicing Catholic since his altar boy days, and although Jenny had no allegiance to any religion whatsoever, for some unknown reason, she decided to give Jack the typical Catholic funeral Mass and burial, followed by a luncheon at one of Jack's favorite Italian restaurants, Puccini's. One of Jack's rules to live by was, "You can always tell a good Italian restaurant by its sauce," something only a non-Italian would say.

It was getting late so we told Jenny we were going to head back to our hotel, but those penetrating eyes of hers caused us to change our plans and join her for late-night coffee and a trip down memory lane at her daughter's house, which was nearby.

Lorraine lived with her husband, Greg, in a well manicured center hall colonial just a few blocks away from the house she grew up in. The first thing that came into view upon entering their beautiful home was a framed poster of her dad, Willy and me. The three of us were standing with our arms around each other, Jack in the middle, Willy to the left, and me on the right. The shot was taken almost twenty-five years ago on the set of *River Rats*, the film that won us our first Academy Award. Lorraine and Greg bid us goodnight and retreated for the evening, leaving Jennifer, Willy, and me gathered around the

The Three Extras

dining room table with a fresh pot of coffee and a plate of chocolate biscotti.

"I miss you guys," Jenny lamented while pouring each of us a cup, "and I'm really going to miss Jack, although for the last couple of years I really can't say he was living, if you know what I mean."

"Hey Jenny, why don't you think about coming down south to live by us," Willy suggested, "Nothing keeping you in California anymore, especially now that Jack's gone."

"Thanks for asking Willy Taylor, I'm not sure what I'm going to do right now. I may just stay with Lorraine until I can sort things out. Let's face it fellows, how much longer until we're worm food?"

"Not me, Jenny Reilly, I ain't feeding no worms," I replied, "I'm getting cremated!"

"Stop it!" Willy chided, "I hate it when you talk like that. We're not going anywhere for a while! We still got a little time left!"

"That's what I've always loved about you, Willy Taylor, always so positive," Jenny said with a heartfelt smile and then tenderly planted a kiss on his cheek. "Do you remember the first time we all met?" she asked.

"Geez," I remarked with a sarcastic grin, "I feel like we're in the senior citizen version of *The Big Chill*. Do you remember that flick?"

"What are you thinking? Taking Jenny upstairs for a quickie?" Willy teased while recalling a scene from the film and reaching for his third biscotti, "These things are freakin' good!"

"Hey, when we first met, I would have jumped at the chance! Jack beat me to it!" I confessed.

"You're so full of it, John Colletti!" Jenny insisted while trying to sidestep the compliment she knew she deserved.

Everybody'd had the hots for Jenny, and why wouldn't they? She was clever, funny, and beautiful.

Quickly changing the subject, Jenny noted, "I'll never forget the time Jack bought his first brand new car. John, do you remember how he wanted to kill us!"

When Japanese cars first emerged on American roadways, they were quite affordable. Jack had purchased a 1971 Toyota Corolla with a manual transmission for less than two thousand dollars. One Saturday afternoon, our group of friends was meeting at the park. Jack and Jen were already there and Jen was sitting in the driver's seat when I arrived. I leaned over to take a peek at the car's interior while Jen was tinkering with the different control knobs and buttons. "What's this?" she asked, as she grabbed onto the choke. I wasn't quite sure what it was either, but always the practical joker, I told her something completely illogical. Neither of us could remember exactly what it was I said, but we did remember the way Jenny yanked the knob so hard that it disengaged from the dashboard. She kept pulling on the cable as if she were reeling in a tuna. When Jack saw the six foot of cable dangling from her hand, he went crazy. "What the hell do you listen to him for?" he screamed, as the two of us couldn't help but laugh uncontrollably. I think it was probably the only time Jack was really angry with me.

Willy and I sat with Jenny for a couple of hours recalling tales of our long- gone youth.

"Where the fuck did the years go?" Jenny sighed, "It's all like a blur!"

"Yeah," I concurred, "It sure went by quick, but we had fun…"

"You know, I guess I couldn't really blame Jack for the Veronica thing. We kind of started taking each other for granted." With her fingertip, Jennifer scattered the chocolate crumbs about on the white table cloth and continued like she had some guilt to unload. "After his heart attack, sex kind of just faded from our lives. Never even talked about it much…sometimes I wish I could go back in time, do things a little differently."

"Don't be so hard on yourself," Willy said sympathetically, "You think it's any different for anybody else. We all just do the best we can. When Tracy died I was so hard on myself, wondering if there was anything I could have done differently, but then I finally realized, hey, this is life, shit happens. I miss her like crazy, but life has to go on."

"We know each other a long, long time," I added, "Not too many people can boast about friendships like we've had. All things considered, we've been pretty blessed." I rose from my chair, collected the empty cups and brought them into the kitchen. "What do you say, Willy? Tomorrow's going to be another long day, let's let this lady get some sleep."

"Joanna trained this guy right, didn't she, Jen?" Willy said, directing her attention to me as I placed the dirty cups into the dishwasher.

"John Colletti, what do you think you're doing? Just leave everything, tomorrow's another day!"

Willy and I each gave Jenny a tight squeeze, told her that we'd see her in the morning and as we walked along the brick pathway towards the driveway, we heard her call out, "I love you Willy Taylor. I love you John Colletti!"

Both of us were emotionally drained and physically exhausted by the time we arrived back at The Marriott, about five miles from Jenny's daughter's place. We stood silently, watching the floor numbers light up one by one until the computerized voice announced that the elevator had arrived at the 10th floor. We stepped out into the corridor and trudged towards our adjoining rooms as if we had weights chained to our ankles. Standing in front of Room 1012, Willy and I gave each other a hug with the intensity of it possibly being our last. I slipped my key card into my door, put on the room light and said, "Good night my friend." Willy took the few steps over to Room 1014 and before I fully closed my door I heard him call out, "I love you, John Colletti!"

After brushing my teeth, I stared intensely into the bathroom mirror and found myself face to face with a man whose thinning silver hair was pulled back into a ponytail, whose almond eyes were surrounded by creases, and whose Adam's apple sported folds of crepey skin spotted with the few hairs he missed with his razor. Jenny's brooding words replayed in my mind, "How the fuck did this happen?" As I pulled down the bedspread of the room's queen-sized bed, I thought about Joanna and the way hotel rooms used to add a little spice to our sex life. It was such a long time ago, yet it seemed like only days since we playfully performed romantic acrobatics upon the sheets. I stacked up a few pillows against the headboard with every intention of sitting up to read for a bit, but my mind was racing and I knew reading would be a waste of time. I wouldn't have retained a word. My thoughts turned to the very reason I was back in New York and sleeping in a hotel room. The reason was Jack. I held the funeral card in my hand, gazing dizzyingly at my friend's name...Jack Reilly, 1952~2037. Feeling as if I'd stepped foot into a time machine, my thoughts spiraled back into the past and I thought about how much I owed to him, how much he had influenced me and how much I was able to accomplish because of him. It was Jack who got me so heavily involved in music, drama and film. It was through Jack I met the girl who gave me my first sexual experience. It was through Jack

I met my wife, Joanna. Most of all, it was only because of Jack's vision that I became part of a world-wide phenomena that has fulfilled my dreams and rewarded me financially. I will go down in cinematic history as one of The Three Extras.

I reached over, turned out the light on the night stand, and then, leaning back, I surrendered to the softness of the pillows and stared up at the ceiling. My emotions were well stirred; I knew there was no way I was going to fall asleep any time soon. A sliver of moonlight shined like a spotlight through a crack in the window blinds, illuminating a corner of the room. As I lay there, physically exhausted but mentally restless, my thoughts seemed to project onto the white ceiling, transforming it into a makeshift cinema screen. I watched intently as scenes from my life chronologically unfolded before me…

John Rullo

~THE DIRTY DISCIPLES~

~It was on an afternoon in late September, 1966, moments before the dismissal bell sounded, when an announcement came over the school's PA system, summoning Jack, Willy, and me to the Dean's office. An announcement like that could have only meant one thing…detention. The three of us entered the dean's office looking like models out of the pages of a teenage fashion magazine, hair glued into place, and clothing just pushing the limits of St. Stanislaw's dress code. I had assumed we were getting bagged for something and my assumption was correct when Brother Joseph James O'Rourke handed each of us a three-day detention slip.

Directing his attention to Willy and Jack, Brother Joe asked, "What were you guys thinking when you got dressed this morning? This is a high school, gents, not a fashion show! I better see you dressed properly tomorrow, and go easy on the hair spray; you guys are fire hazards."

With their heads bowed down like repentant sinners, Willy and Jack conceded in harmony, "Yes, Brother."

"Colletti!" the dean hollered, "And what do you think you were doing? I know that wasn't a hearing aid in your ear during history class!"

I couldn't believe I actually got caught listening to the radio in class. I pretended to play dumb when Brother Joe backhanded me against my breast pocket and discovered my transistor radio attached to an earphone. I was busted. He confiscated it and told me he would return it to me in June.

The Three Extras

"I'll see the three of you in detention hall at three o'clock," he ordered, as we left his office with our tails between our legs.

Although we weren't the least bit happy about having to serve detention, we were ecstatic over not one of us being told to get a haircut. Willy's offense was wearing a shocking blue Nehru jacket. School policy was that blazers required lapels and or collars. Jack's misdeed was wearing boots with three-inch Cuban heels, definitely not regulation. If it weren't for the metal taps he applied to them, he may have gotten away with it. As for me, I was obsessed with The Rolling Stones, and up until that afternoon, always had my radio on, anxiously awaiting the next time "Get Off Of My Cloud" would play.

For the next three days, Jack, Willy and I sat side by side in the dreaded Room 105, Detention Hall, and it was there where a lifelong friendship began. Although talking was prohibited, every time the teacher who was assigned to monitor the small group of delinquents left the room, we chatted away as if there were no tomorrow. We talked about everything under the sun during those three eternal afternoons, but music was the one subject we were most passionate about. We discovered that each of us played an instrument and on Jack's suggestion, the following weekend we gathered together in Willy's parents' garage and formed a band. Willy's favorite band was The Dave Clark Five. When he discovered that Dave Clark was actually the drummer, he decided he wanted to play the drums. Unlike Jack and me, Willy was a natural, never took a lesson, had a great sense of rhythm and developed into quite the percussionist. Jack had been taking guitar lessons since grade school, but ever since he saw Paul McCartney plucking away on his Hofner bass, he became fascinated with the instrument and decided to take up the bass. My grandfather played guitar, and from the time I was a little kid, I admired the way he could entertain himself. He would give me a lesson now and then and when my parents saw how much I loved it, they decided to bring me for lessons from a real teacher.

We were all just beginners on our instruments, but we had determination and decent singing voices. We did our best to cover songs by the Beatles, the Stones, and many of the other early British Invasion bands. We named our group "The Dirty Disciples," Jack's idea, and before long we had a repertoire of almost thirty songs and got our first paying gig at George Watson's fifteenth birthday party. George's dad paid us fifty bucks and everybody who was at the celebration thought we sounded great, or at least that's what they told us! I can't imagine how we could have sounded anything other than awful, singing through the cheap microphones we had plugged into our Sears guitar amps with Willy pounding on drums and cymbals with tones just slightly better than cardboard boxes and stainless steel pot covers. Whatever the case, that night, the few girls who attended were glued to our sides and in just a matter of days, word spread throughout the corridors of St. Stanislaw's that Jack, Willy, and I were members of a rock 'n roll band, making us the three coolest kids in the school.

One afternoon as we swaggered like rock stars towards the school cafeteria, we were intercepted by Mr. Mulroney, one of a small number of lay teachers at St. Stanislaw's and director of the drama department. "Mr. Taylor, Mr. Colletti, and Mr. Reilly, please come to my office after school today, there's something I'd like to discuss with you!"

The first thought that came to my mind was we were all headed for detention again, but when we entered his office that same afternoon, my fear quickly vanished. "Gentlemen," he said, "Kindly take a seat!"

"Thanks, Mr. M," Jack said, acting as our spokesman. "What can we do for you?"

"Well, boys, the question is, what can we do for each other? Have any of you ever considered joining the Drama Club and auditioning for a school play?"

"Aw, come on Mr. Mulroney," Jack replied, almost as if the question were an insult, "Drama's for fag…uh, I mean, geeks!"

"Oh yeah," Mr. Reilly, "Are you telling me Marlon Brando was a geek?"

"You're talking high school play, Mr. M, not Broadway!" Jack shot back.

"Hey, he had to get his start somewhere! But forget about Brando for a minute. Do you guys have any idea of how you're looked up to in this school? The three of you have an aura that demands attention. I can see it in your walk, the way you handle yourselves. Having the three of you in the cast of one of our performances would not only pack the auditorium, it would get a lot of the other students interested in drama…not just the fag, uh, I mean, geeks!"

The three of us looked at each other, shrugging our shoulders indecisively as Mr. Mulroney tried his very best to sell us.

"Okay, you think about it, but as you do, consider this…St. Stanislaw's is an all boy school. The only extracurricular activity that allows interaction with girls is the Drama Club. The girls from Blessed Redeemer High School participate in all of our productions, and let me remind you, gentlemen, some of those ladies are very cute! Mull it over and let me know by Friday."

Sitting in our customary seats at the back of the bus on the way home from school that same day, Jack made the decision for us. "Dirty Disciples," he announced, "We're gonna be actors and we're gonna meet chicks!"

The last thing Willy and I wanted to do was to take part in a school activity that required us to hang out at school even longer than we had to. Committing to drama, however, meant staying late after school and forfeiting a few weekends for rehearsals, but with the prospect of meeting girls, we conceded. Prior to auditions for the next production, Mr. Mulroney had secretly made arrangements with the three of us. He requested that we go through the motions and try out just like any other student, but no matter what, we were guaranteed parts.

Just as we suspected, most of the boys who had showed up with high hopes of landing roles were far from what we considered cool. It was obvious they took acting quite seriously as they performed scenes from *Macbeth, Death of a Salesman, Streetcar Named Desire*, and other classic plays. Jack, Willy, and I patiently tolerated the excruciatingly boring auditions of our classmates, because sitting directly behind us were at least two dozen girls from Blessed Redeemer who had come, via school bus, to St. Stanislaw's to hopefully participate in our production of *Murder in the Cathedral*.

Mr. Mulroney stood in front of the stage holding a clipboard in his hand, taking meticulous notes on each student's performance. Looking up, he called out Jack's name, "Mr. Reilly, let's see what you've got!"

Jack rose from his seat and before responding to the director, turned to us and whispered, "Ready, boys?"

He made his way out of the aisle and assertively walked towards the stage. In a manner much the same as that of an over-confident lawyer, Jack pointed a finger at Mr. Mulroney and said, "I know this may be a bit out of the ordinary, but assuming

The Three Extras

you would approve, John, Willy and I have decided to perform a scene together."

Not knowing what to expect, Mulroney cautiously nodded in approval. Jack motioned for Willy and I to join him center stage where we proceeded to perform a slapstick routine from a Three Stooges episode. Jack took on the role of Moe, grabbing Willy by the hair and barking, "Hey, Porcupine, what's the matter with you?" Playing the part of Curly, I laughed, "Nyuck, nyuck, nyuck!" only to get reprimanded from Moe, who, while poking me in the eyes and hitting me on the head, shouted, "What's so funny, you lame brain?" The girls were laughing hysterically as we improvised our way through a routine we had seen so many times it was like second nature to us. Mr. M rolled his eyes and huffed, as if to say, "Come on guys, at least pretend to take this seriously!"

Although none of us landed the lead role in the play, the three of us were cast in minor roles with minimal lines to memorize. That suited us just fine! We were the last of the boys to audition but all of us were asked to remain seated in the auditorium to give the girls support until they completed their try-outs. That was the afternoon when we first met Jennifer.

Dressed in her blue and green plaid skirt, white cotton blouse, and black oxford loafers, Jenny boldly approached us and said, "Hey, you guys were great up there; unconventional but funny as shit!" Jenny stood out from all her colleagues; she was ravishingly gorgeous, in fact, I noticed her the second the girls entered the auditorium and thought to myself, "Hey, this just may turn out to be alright!" If she looked that good in a regulation uniform, I could only imagine what she would have looked like in jeans.

"Hi, I'm Jennifer Mancuso," she said with a smile, which I wanted to believe was a bit flirtatious.

I answered first. "Hi Jennifer, I'm John Colletti," then turning to my comrades, I said, "And this is Moe and Larry!"

Jennifer laughed out loud and before I had the opportunity to say another word, Jack yanked me by the arm and in his best Moe voice cried out, "I ought to mutilate you, pudding head!" Before I knew it, they were standing face to face and he formally introduced himself, "Hi, Jennifer, I'm Jack Reilly and the third stooge is Willy Taylor."

"Very nice to meet you Jack Reilly, Willy Taylor, and John Colletti," she said with one of the prettiest smiles I had ever seen.

Even though the three of us were thoroughly taken by her charms, it was easy to deduce how she had eyes for Jack, politely ignoring Willy and me and devoting most of her attention to him. Willy and I got the hint and left the two of them alone while we unsuccessfully scoped the room for other possibilities.

From that day on, Jenny and Jack, a very handsome couple, became an item, which in turn made Jenny, Jack, Willy and me an item, because as she quickly discovered, nobody comes between The Dirty Disciples. Jennifer was enthralled with the idea of hanging out with a rock band and even more so that she was dating one of its members. As it turned out, she didn't aspire to be an actress. She was assigned to the costume design team, so there was no need for her to be present every day, making rehearsals a little less intimidating and a lot less distracting.

Jack had a natural stage presence and great diction. As director, Mr. Mulroney wanted the dialogue to sound authentic by having the actors and actresses deliver their lines with the best British accents we could muster up. Jack had no problem, but Willy and I could not elude our Queens, New York accents no matter how hard we tried. We were cast as three of the four priests. Mr. Mulroney was getting frustrated with our inability to produce what sounded even vaguely like British accents and then he had a brainstorm. As if he had a glimpse into the future and foresaw the troubles facing the Catholic Church, he suggested that Willy and I go about playing the roles as gay priests, coaching us to speak in a highly exaggerated, stereotypical, effeminate tone of voice. At the time, we were a bit immature regarding such matters, so initially we were a little uncomfortable about doing so; but since it added some comic relief to a dark, ominous script, we obliged him.

Murder in the Cathedral was a huge success, and just as Mr. Mulroney suspected, due to the draw of The Dirty Disciples, all three performances were standing room only. The audience roared as Willy and I gave it our best, with campy renditions of blatantly homosexual priests, complete with lisp. Although it wasn't very fair to our fellow cast members, whenever Jack, Willy, or I stepped onto the stage, our personal cheering sections went wild with deafening applause.

The three of us remained in the drama club throughout high school, partially because Jenny did, partially because Willy and I hoped to find our very own Jenny, partially because we loved the attention, and partially because we felt a sense of loyalty to Mr. Mulroney. There were many times, due to his interceding, we escaped the torment of detention. We performed in four other productions after *Murder*, always in minor roles, except for the one time in which Jack was given the lead as Tully Bascombe in *The Mouse That Roared*. I have to admit, belonging to the Drama Club made attending an all-boy Catholic high school somewhat more bearable, and although we didn't know it at the time, it actually paved the path for the rest of our lives.

One of the perks of belonging to the Drama Club was the cast parties that usually took place on the first Saturday night following each production's final performance. These gatherings of performers, stage crew, costume and set designers, make-up artists, and promotional staff happened at the homes of volunteering parents. It was sophomore year and once again, the play was a smashing success with three sold-out performances, partly due to our popularity and charisma. The cast party was being held at the home of Margaret Quinn, a senior at Blessed Redeemer and one of the set designers. She lived in a big beautiful three-story house located on the Long Island Sound in the well-to-do village of Douglaston. As soon as I entered, I could smell money! There was a Steinway grand piano in the center of their living room, sculptures and paintings situated about, décor unlike that of any house I'd ever been in. Mr. and Mrs. Quinn met each guest at the door, assuring all the parents who were dropping off their kids that they were in good hands. Jack had just gotten his learner's permit and somehow convinced his folks that it was perfectly legal for him to be driving with Jennifer, Willy and me as passengers, provided he didn't leave the state! I guess Willy and I, likewise, convinced our parents it was perfectly safe getting into a car with Jack behind the wheel. Looking back, I could never be sure if what we used to get away with was because we were so sly or because our parents were too exhausted to care!

The Quinns directed everyone downstairs to a beautifully finished basement complete with state of the art audio equipment, recessed lighting and dozens of framed movie posters on all the walls. They seemed much younger and hipper than my folks. Mr. Quinn had long hair and sideburns and Mrs. Quinn fit very nicely into her faded bell-bottom Levis.

The Three Extras

"You kids have a great time," they instructed, "Margaret, if you need anything, we'll be upstairs."

At previous cast parties, it was customary for drama students to chip in for beverages and snacks while parents would join forces and prepare assorted trays of food. Margaret's parents had the party catered and paid for everything. There was hot food, heroes, salads, desserts, snacks, and for the first time ever, beer. A few of the nerdy kids got a little uptight when they saw the alcohol, but they just kept to themselves, huddled in a corner, and ate to their hearts' content. Jack and Jennifer were attached at the hip, so Willy and I each indulged in a beer then decided to go our separate ways and mingle.

I rarely talked to Margaret during any of the productions, yet we had always acknowledged one another with a smile or a nod. She was kind of pretty, fair skinned with a few freckles, greenish-blue eyes, and long straight blond hair. She was comparatively tall, maybe five feet, eight inches, still shorter than my six feet. She was so much more attractive when she wasn't wearing that hideous school uniform. Seeing her that evening in low cut jeans and a black V-neck sweater made me quite attentive to her every move. Maybe she became aware that I had taken notice of her, I wasn't sure, but she broke the ice by coming over to me and asking, "Hey, I hear you're in a band. Is that true?"

I loved talking about our band so I answered, "Yeah, you know Jack Reilly and Willy Taylor? The three of us are in a band called The Dirty Disciples!"

"What instrument do you play?" she asked.

I don't know if it was my imagination, but I wanted to believe I sensed a little flirtation in her voice when I replied, "Guitar, I play guitar."

"Who's your favorite band?" she inquired as she bit down on her bottom lip, a move that struck me as extremely erotic.

"The Stones," I said without giving her question much thought, "Definitely the Rolling Stones."

She told me that although she liked the Stones, she preferred the Beatles and George was her favorite. "You know, you kind of look a bit like George. Did anybody ever tell you that?"

"No," I said, feeling as if I were just given a huge compliment, "You're the first!"

"Hey, you want to take a walk?" she asked with a hint of playful mischief in her voice, "I want you to hear something!"

It was a beautiful spring evening. The two of us made our way through a small corridor leading to the exit to the backyard. The night sky was filled with stars that sparkled like diamonds while the light of the three quarter moon skimmed the surface of the sound's still water. She led the way along the deck, passing by her dad's boat, a vehicle bigger than some of my friends' houses, and motioned for me to follow her towards the garage. My curiosity overcame my hesitance and I obeyed her orders, trailing directly behind her until we arrived at the rear of the garage. She lifted a patio block revealing the key that unlocked the mystery door which led to a flight of steps. Shutting the door behind us, she signaled me to go up and followed me to the top. She reached around me and turned a switch providing just enough dim light for us to find our way around. I assumed we were in her dad's office. There was a desk, a couple of leather recliners, and a matching couch. There was a free-standing shelving system that held a stereo and stacks of record albums. I couldn't help but sense I was trespassing, but she assured me she's done this before and just wanted to turn me on to some records. Displayed on the wall was a grouping of family photos, including the Quinns' wedding picture and it occurred to me that they appeared too young to have a daughter who was a senior in high school. Margaret noticed I was studying the photos and she knew my questions before I had even asked. She explained how she was legally adopted by the couple in the photo, her real dad's younger brother and his wife. Margaret's natural parents were both killed in an automobile accident and so her aunt and uncle became her adopted parents. Although I found the situation and the events to be tragic and very out of the ordinary, it shed a light on how she had such young parents and so I didn't dare to ask any further questions.

    I stared in amazement at her dad's outstanding record collection. She was on her knees flipping through the hundreds of records just like they were files in a rolodex, pulling out certain ones and placing them down beside her. "Check these out," she said excitedly, as if she had unearthed the Dead Sea Scrolls, and handed me albums by bands such as Quicksilver Messenger Service, Jefferson Airplane, Moby Grape, Country Joe and the Fish and the Grateful Dead. "Check this one out," she insisted, passing me the album jacket to a record called *Electric Music for the Mind and Body* by Country Joe and the Fish. She carefully placed the vinyl onto the turntable and said, "You're gonna love this…." All the mentioned bands came out of San Francisco and, being the music lover I was, I was surprised that I had never heard of any of them. She told me that Mr. Quinn had a business associate who would give him records even before they were released assuring him that these bands were going to be the next big thing. I was immediately turned on to what I was listening to and couldn't wait to enlighten my band mates. Margaret reached for the brown cigar box that was sitting upon her dad's desk, opened the lid and pulled out what was undoubtedly a marijuana cigarette. "You smoke pot, don't you?" she asked.

I had never smoked pot; in fact, I had never even smoked a cigarette, but I wasn't about to let this girl think I was a square. "Of course, I do," I answered, slightly paranoid of what I imagined could possibly happen. I had heard so often about how smoking pot eventually led to heroin addiction and for a moment I saw myself strung out in an alley trying desperately to plunge a needle into my collapsed purple veins!

She walked over to the rear window and opened it slightly, allowing the fresh salt water breeze to enter the room. She lit the joint, took the first hit, and passed it over to me. I put the thin, wrinkled, strange looking cigarette to my virgin lips, inhaled quick and deeply, and tried desperately not to choke. I choked. I choked, and I choked some more.

"Are you okay?" she asked sympathetically as she chuckled simultaneously.

"I'm, I'm fine," I tried to assure her while hacking between every syllable.

By the time I took my third hit, I was getting the hang of it, no longer gagging, feeling its pleasurable effects. Margaret looked over at me, smiled, and proposed we dance. "What if we get caught up here?" I asked in a fleeting moment of paranoia.

"Relax, nobody's going to catch us, Johnny Boy," she said slowly and convincingly, "Nobody's going to catch us."

Feeling as if my legs were rubber, I rose to my feet and met Margaret on the dance floor. We leaned into each others' bodies, put our arms around each other, and swayed to the psychedelic sounds of Country Joe and the Fish's *Not So Sweet Martha Lorraine*, kissing each other softly in rhythm to the music. Margaret's right hand slowly inched down landing squarely between my legs and I got the sneaking feeling I was about to experience another first. All the saints in heaven were aghast and my guardian angel was warning me to flee from the lures of sin, but I was too stoned to do anything other than surrender to the pleasure.

I imagined I must have been pretty high. I could feel the smile on my face stretching and stretching like taffy and I envisioned myself appearing like a circus clown with mascara-lined squinty eyes, white-face and red nose. We both started to giggle as she shifted her weight onto me. Unable to hold her up, I fell backwards and together we seemed to float gracefully into the waiting recliner. Margaret's hand never left my crotch as she slithered along my body like a serpent, dropping to her knees and burying her face in my lap. In my euphoric state, I paid no heed to my Catholic boy guilt and watched as Margaret unzipped my jeans and proceeded to treat me to my very first sexual encounter. I never imagined my body was capable of feeling such intense pleasure and as I laid there trembling in a newfound indefinable ecstasy, I didn't know what part of me was going to explode first; my heart, my brain or the part Margaret was tending to so lovingly. It turned out that my heart and brain remained intact. When the task of corrupting my innocence was complete, she quickly peeled off her jeans and pink polka dot panties and pulled me down to join her on the shag carpeting. As I lay on top of her, she wriggled her way up, firmly pushed my head downward and whispered, "Now you can return the favor!" As inexperienced as they come, there I was with my nose in a triangular patch of curly blond hair, face to face with my first real live vagina. After poking around for a few seconds and with her patient guidance, I figured out what I was expected to do and got busy while Margaret moaned with delight, *Happiness Is a Porpoise Mouth* playing in the background.

Immediately after I accomplished what she had set out for me to do, she speedily got dressed, I zipped up and we listened to a few more cuts from the albums she had selected. By that time we had both straightened out considerably. Ready and anxious for a repeat performance, I reached for her hand but she quickly pulled away and said, "We had better get back before someone comes searching for us!" I reluctantly agreed; she put everything back where it belonged and as we made our way back to the house she acted as if nothing ever happened.

Back at the party I hooked up with Jack, Willy, and Jennifer again and Willy asked, "Where the hell have you been, I've been looking all over for you?"

"You're not gonna believe it when I tell you, man, you're not gonna believe a word of it!"

When the party finally broke, I made it a point to say goodnight to Margaret hoping that maybe I could see her again. Her attention seemed to be on everyone but me. I was completely dumbfounded. How did we do what we just did and pretend it never happened. When she finally had no choice but to face me, all she could say was, "Hope you liked the music," then turned away. As the four of us walked towards Jack's car, I was lost in thought, detached from everything and everyone around me, wondering if the love of my life had any idea that she had just taken me from ecstasy to desolation, shattering both my heart and my ego.

As I sat despondent in the back seat next to Willy, with his curiosity aroused, he drilled me, "Okay, where the fuck did you disappear to?"

I made my confession. When I finished telling my three companions all about how Margaret turned me on to pot, oral sex, and Country Joe and the Fish, without batting an eyelid Willy said, "Fuck you, you're lying!"

Even though I was brokenhearted and bewildered, I managed to smile and said, "I told you that you wouldn't believe me!"

Jennifer, laughing from the front seat beside Jack, remarked, "You're such a good story teller, John Colletti!"

After that ever-so-memorable night, I never saw her again. She graduated and went off to college, and I became a junior. Due to my twisted Catholic upbringing, I went through a very brief period thinking God was disappointed in me for committing some disgusting sin of sexual deviancy, but I soon got over it. Margaret had opened up a whole new world for me; sex, drugs, and exciting new rock 'n roll. The only haunting question plaguing me for a while was, "Am I still a virgin?"

John Rullo

~ELECTRIC DUST~

    I managed to find copies of those great albums Margaret had played for me in a record store in Manhattan's East Village. I called a meeting of my band mates and had them sit and listen to each and every one. Just as I suspected, they were as turned on as I was, so we immediately decided to revamp our repertoire by replacing the British pop with San Francisco psychedelic. We changed the name of the band to Electric Dust and once again, we established ourselves as the coolest guys in St. Stanislaw's. We started our own little promotional campaign by etching the letters E D I C on the back of every desk we could. Until word leaked out, we were the only ones who had any idea that E D I C stood for Electric Dust Is Coming.

    We added another member to the band. He was a guitarist named Frank Acuri who lived directly around the corner from Willy. One Saturday afternoon, he heard us rehearsing and came knocking on Willy's garage door. He was very hip to the music we covered and practically begged if he could jam with us. Jack had been saying for some time that several of our songs were sounding a bit empty and had often suggested the addition of keyboards or another guitar to fill out our sound and allow us to be more creative. He insisted we oblige Frank by letting him try out. Frank was home and back with his gear in seconds flat. He plugged his Fender Mustang into his Deluxe Reverb amplifier and immediately we clicked. Frank looked like a rock star. He didn't attend a Catholic school so he didn't have any dress codes to adhere to. His curly black hair extended down past his shoulders and he could play guitar better than anyone we knew, including me. The satisfied smile on Jack's face signaled us that Frank was in. As far as we could tell, we were the only band in Queens playing predominantly San Francisco rock.

Jack's older brother, Eddie, had a good friend named Roger who owned a club on Utopia Parkway in Bayside called The Courthouse. They featured live music every Friday and Saturday night, and even though we were minors, Eddie guaranteed us he could land us a gig there. We had come a long way since George Watson's birthday party. The following year for Christmas, Santa left Willy a genuine set of Ludwig drums with Zildjian cymbals; Jack had saved up enough to purchase a second hand Ampeg bass amp and a slightly used Fender Jazz bass guitar; and I acquired a Gibson SG along with a Fender Twin Reverb amplifier from an older cousin who gave up on music and joined the Navy. Our new member, Frank, inherited a pro PA system from his previous band, so we were set to go! Eddie was pretty cool and very supportive of his brother's musical endeavors. He often volunteered his services to drive the band and our equipment to and from gigs in his work van. When he was unable to be there, he let Jack take the van in spite of the fact he only had a learner's permit.

The Courthouse crew loved Electric Dust, maybe not so much for the style of music we played, but for the way we packed the place. Back in those more innocent times, bar owners paid little or no attention to the rules, so all of our underage fans were able to get in to see and hear us perform under the stipulation they each bought a beer or two. The Courthouse was twice the size of most of the local bars. On the club's far right was a stage, large enough to accommodate a fully equipped band. On the far left was a horseshoe shaped bar with a full view of the stage. Along the walls were booths where couples usually stowed away for the night to make out. The club was very dark, its walls and ceilings painted flat black, the front windows tinted, and the only light, coming from the hanging neon beer signs and the purplish black lights, gave everyone in the place a ghost-like appearance. Only God knows the tiny creatures that were very likely to have been crawling about on the floor in the shadows.

The club had us back so often, it became our home away from home. Every week our fan base grew and best of all, we were getting paid. The word spread rather quickly about the psychedelic music we became so proficient at playing, and before long, our popularity spread to the local colleges. We became too cool for our own good.

We created quite a few memories at The Courthouse. One summer evening in between sets, I walked out to the parking lot to escape the irritating fumes of the cigarette smoke filling the bar. I was alone in thought, sitting on the hood of my car, when a girl who had been watching the band rather intently approached me.

"Hey! You guys sound pretty good," she complimented, "Good to hear a band play something other than that Top 40 shit!"

I acknowledged her accolade with a smile and said, "Thanks, glad you like it!"

She moved a bit closer and situated herself squarely between my knees. Her face nearly touching mine, I could smell the sweetness of her perfume as she introduced herself. "Hi, I'm Valerie. I've seen you guys play here a few times!"

Valerie was interestingly pretty. She had droopy dark brown eyes which made it appear as if she were a little stoned. Her long black hair was unruly and somewhat wavy probably due to the dampness in the air. Her two front teeth overlapped ever so slightly which added to the cuteness of her smile and her lips were full and soft. I reached out to shake her hand and told her my name, "Hi Valerie, I'm John, John Colletti!"

Valerie was wearing skin tight black jeans and a white-cotton button-down men's dress shirt, which was unbuttoned about a quarter of the way down. She wasn't wearing a bra and every time she moved it was like playing "hide and seek" with the milky white breasts that contrasted with her summer tan. Valerie's fingers reached down into her shirt pocket and pulled out a half-smoked joint and a book of matches. "Care to join me?" she asked.

"Well, maybe just a hit," I answered after she had already lit up.

Watching her lips caress the tip of the joint sent a rush through my entire body as I thought about the last time I had gotten high with a girl.

We passed it back and forth just a couple of times until I told her I couldn't get too wasted because I had to get back inside to play. She snuffed out the roach and placed it back into her pocket. I was a little buzzed and before I knew it, her arms were around me pulling me closer until we were locked at the lips. As if my hands had a mind of their own, they wandered about under her shirt until they rested on her breasts. Slowly her head made the much anticipated descent. I leaned back and allowed her to do what she set out to do. Seconds after treating me to what was a much unexpected surprise, I heard Willy's voice call out, "Johnny! We've gotta get back on!"

Valerie smiled, kissed me quickly and said, "Dedicate a song to me, okay?"

Just before we broke into the first song of the next set, from behind the drums, Willy called out, "What the hell were you doing out there, Johnny boy?"

"You wouldn't believe it if I told you, Willy!"

Valerie split before we had finished our last set, and just like it was with Margaret, ours was a brief affair...very brief...once! The next time I saw her she'd introduced me to her college boyfriend and I still hadn't lost my virginity.

Thanks to Margaret and Valerie, I was completely misled into thinking the sexual favors I received were nothing out of the ordinary and it was just what girls did to circumvent having intercourse and risk pregnancy. Man, was I delusional. A few slaps in the face and cries of "You sick bastard!" with future girls cleared that misconception up rather quickly.

While we were packing up our equipment that evening, Willy grabbed me by the arm and asked, "Hey Johnny, who was that girl I saw you with in the parking lot earlier?"

Once again I didn't hide the truth, "Oh, you mean Valerie? We got high and kind of had sex!"

Once again he replied, "You're such a fuckin' liar."

We were scheduled to play yet another weekend at The Clubhouse. As much as we loved performing at our home away from home, we felt as if we needed to branch out and appear at other venues. It was exciting news when Jack informed us that Roger told Eddie about a new venue in Flushing called The Bee Hive. According to Eddie, The Bee Hive was looking for warm-up bands to open for up and coming major acts, such as The Blues Magoos and The Grateful Dead, and Roger thought we would be perfect. Naturally, we were very excited over the prospect of meeting some of the bands we emulated. Arrangements were made to have the manager of The Bee Hive come down to The Clubhouse on Friday night to check us out.

Frank was screwing up in school. He had failed a couple of subjects and his dad told him that until his grades picked up,

The Three Extras

he was no longer permitted to play with Electric Dust. He unhappily notified us that he wouldn't be able to play with the band on the night of the audition. We were devastated upon hearing the news, but then Jack got a hold of Frank and told him, "I don't care what you have to do, even if it means drugging your parents, you had better be at the club Friday night!"

Well, Frank took Jack literally when he ground up sleeping pills and spiked his parents' customary after-dinner pot of coffee. Both his mom and dad had passed out on the couch and remained there until the following morning with no clue they were drugged by their own son just so he could sneak out of the house and make it to an audition. The following afternoon, Jack stopped by Frank's house pretending to be upset over the news of our guitar player being grounded. Instead of pleading, Jack tried bargaining with Mr. Acuri. In an attempt to get Mr. Acuri to allow Frank to continue playing with the band, Jack offered to tutor Frankie with his schoolwork. If his grades didn't improve by the next marking period, Frank would have no choice but to give up the band. We didn't know if it was because the Acuri's were still under the numbing effects of the drug or because they assumed since Jack went to private school he was smart. Whatever the reason, it bought the band time.

In spite of the "edge of our seat" tension and stress associated with Frankie's timely escape from his parents' imprisonment, the audition went great. We were booked to play The Bee Hive as opening act for the Grateful Dead, who, although we idolized them, were relatively unknown at the time outside of the San Francisco area. They were travelling about the country in a van and somehow found their way to Flushing, Queens.

Surprisingly, the club wasn't as packed as we assumed it would be. Most of our fans could see us on any weekend at The Clubhouse for free, so they weren't about to pay a cover charge to see a relatively unknown San Francisco band, even though Electric Dust did a pretty good version of "Morning Dew." We went over well with the much older crowd, but the most thrilling thing for us was to be hanging out "backstage," a small dank storage room adjacent to the kitchen, with the members of The Grateful Dead. Little did we know that Jerry Garcia would one day become a rock legend. Hearing the band relate a few road stories, most of them centering on being in an altered state of some kind, certainly impressed four inexperienced minors who hadn't ventured outside of Queens. When the night was over, we told them how exciting it was to have met them and how we looked forward to playing together again sometime. Somehow that never happened.

Jack had unanimously been appointed manager of the band. After all, it was because of his skills in diplomacy that Frank was able to continue playing with us, and Jack's brother Eddie was the one getting us gigs. We figured it would be best to let Jack handle anything related to band finances, including seeing that we got paid. Jimmy, the owner of the Bee Hive, tried to stiff us that night. He had seemed like a decent guy. In fact, if I hadn't had known any better, I would have mistaken him for another member of the Dead. He was unshaven and wore his dirty blond hair long, straggly and unkempt. His jeans were completely frayed at the bottom, the strands of tattered denim hanging over his Keds high top sneakers, and the Beatles' logo on his black tee shirt was fading from either over-washing or over-wearing.

The Three Extras

After Jerry, Pigpen, Phil, Bob and the rest of the Dead had disappeared somewhere, we had packed up our gear, Jimmy came over to talk with us.

"Hey, you guys sounded pretty fuckin' good tonight! Any of you ever trip?"

Jack, being our spokesman, answered, "I almost broke my neck on the curb outside when we unloaded earlier…"

Jimmy laughed, uncertain of whether or not Jack was putting him on, and said, "No, I meant have you guys ever tried acid? Judging from the way you fellows play, I would have to assume you did!"

"Yeah, we tried it a couple of times," Jack lied, not wanting Jimmy to think we weren't cool.

"Listen guys," Jimmy began his negotiations, "Because I had agreed to pay The Grateful Dead so much, I really can't afford to pay you guys in cash, but I can give you this and a promise to get you some future gigs," as he handed Jack five tabs of acid and a dime bag of marijuana.

At the moment, it never occurred to Jack, or any of us for that matter, that we had the upper hand. We could have easily pressured Jimmy for the money by threatening to report him for hiring underage musicians and trying to compensate them with illegal drugs, but then we realized if we did so, we might never work as a band again. Jack accepted Jimmy's payment. Until then, I was the only one who had ever dabbled in smoking pot. That night, we all indulged and the world as we knew it changed.

In the wee hours of the morning, with mixed emotions, the four of us sat in the van still parked outside the Bee Hive. We were ecstatic over the fact we got to meet and play with The Grateful Dead, but we were bummed out about not getting paid with real money.

"What the fuck are we supposed to do with this shit," Willy complained, referring to the weed and the LSD.

"Well, we can smoke the pot," I suggested.

"Since when do you smoke marijuana," Jack asked curiously surprised.

"I've been trying to tell you guys, but you don't want to believe me…"

"You mean those stories with the girls and the pot and the sex were true?" Willy sputtered.

"Hey," I calmly replied, "Why would I lie?"

Jack tossed me the brown envelope containing the pot and said, "It's about time I try this shit. Do what you have to do!"

I asked Frank for one of his cigarettes and, placing it between my fingers, I delicately rolled it, removing the tobacco. I then carefully refilled the empty cigarette with weed. I pulled off the filter and twisted both ends. Frank lit a match and held it up to my face. The flame met the tip of the makeshift joint, smoke floated towards the van's interior light and the paper burned a bright orange as I inhaled. After taking a long hit, I passed it over to Willy. We huddled together in what amounted to a tribal ceremony and before the magic cigarette could no longer be held by our fingertips, we were all pleasantly stoned.

As the months rolled along into years, I have to say, it was good to be us. Everybody wanted to be our friends. Because of our vital role in the drama club, Mr. Mulroney pressured the administration to give us an unusual amount of slack. Our continued appearance in school plays resulted in record-breaking attendances. Miraculously, Frank's grades improved and Electric Dust became as popular as ever when FM radio emerged, transmitting psychedelic music over the airwaves helping it to quickly catch on. Jimmy kept his promise and got us some pretty good gigs in trendy Manhattan clubs. Two of our better shows were when we opened up for the Blues Magoos at the Gaslight Café and The Electric Prunes at The Bitter End in Manhattan's Greenwich Village, the East Coast haven for hippies, artists and free-thinkers. The Magoos later had a hit called "We Ain't Got Nothing Yet" and The Prunes were known for "I Had Too Much to Dream Last Night." After meeting both bands, we felt it would be cool to learn their songs and add them into our set lists. Jack, Willy and I were Catholic high school kids from the uptight suburbs of Queens living many of our weekends as if we actually were rock stars.

In the spring of 1969, we were nearing the end of our junior year. The band had an informal practice on a Saturday afternoon and we tried to come up with some new material. Jack and Jenny had fallen very much in love, and more times than not, she was hanging out with us. It was nice having a pretty female face among the group. It was a warm, partly sunny day so we decided to take a break and walk over to nearby Bowne Park. As the five of us sat in a circle on resurrected green grass, Jack reached into his pocket and pulled out a small white envelope. He was still holding on to the five tabs of acid from the night at the Bee Hive. Ever since we had all gotten stoned together in the van, we had talked about trying LSD but never had the nerve or the opportunity.

"What do you say?" he proposed, "Any better time than now?"

Skeptical, Willy reached out his hand and said, "Let me see that stuff." Jack placed the tiny tab of yellow-stained paper into his palm and Willy stared at it. "I can't believe that swallowing this speck of paper is going to make me hallucinate!"

We had heard quite a few "bad trip" stories: a tale about a kid who thought he could fly and jumped out of a ten-story window to his death and another about a girl who had imagined she was on fire and dove into a river and drowned. We decided that should we partake, one of us would abstain to avert tragedy. Jack tried to convince his girlfriend not to indulge, but she was adamant about sharing in the experience. After about twenty minutes of stalling, arguing and trying to reach a decision about who was not going to take the drug, Frank volunteered.

Jack, Willy, Jenny and I each held the minuscule fragment of paper in our hands, and as if we were toasting champagne glasses, raised our arms, placed the paper onto our tongues and then waited. I couldn't say for sure how much time elapsed before feeling the effects, but there was no mistaking that something was happening. Initially, everything around me became distorted and elongated, as if I was looking into a fun house mirror at a carnival. I could see Frank's words leave his lips, his voice, gravelly, deep and in slow motion. Asking if we were alright, each syllable sounded like a 45 being played at 16 RPM. Everything surrounding me appeared big, bright and beautiful. Willy was sitting to my left and as the sun rays beamed down upon him, he glowed like a golden statue, his hair taking on the look of a lion's mane. Laughing squirrels scurried about looking like characters from Disney cartoons and clouds were perched upon the treetops like huge puffs of cotton candy. Jenny sat to my right radiating like a heavenly angel. We were each holding hands with the ones sitting beside us and I felt as if our flesh was melding. I sensed a spiritual energy surging through me, entering me from the right and leaving from the left in a continuous flow, giving me the sensation we were all one entity.

The Three Extras

The air steadily became cooler as the sun, losing its intensity, began its daily descent. Gradually, I returned to the tedious, lackluster reality I had temporarily escaped. I had to admit, my first acid trip was a rather pleasant experience. When everyone seemed to have their feet back on the ground, we strolled back to Willy's house, each of us trying our best to describe what we had just undergone. It was amazing to discover how different each of our experiences was. Jenny's was similar to mine; she spoke of multicolored, animated surroundings and feelings of inner peace. Willy said, for him, everything seemed to move in a jerky motion, the way things appear when under a strobe light. Jack, however, was quiet. He gave the impression he didn't care to share his thoughts. Jenny kept pressing him until he finally told us he would probably never trip again. What he envisioned while under the influence was quite the opposite of his comrades. Jack admitted to feeling frightened; he described birds appearing like demons, the sky losing its color and turning a dark shade of gray while the voices around him sounded raspy and evil. He didn't want to talk about it any further so we didn't pursue it.

I can't say for certain it was from the effects of the acid, but ever since that afternoon in the park, something inside me I believe had long been sealed tightly shut, opened wide. It was as if something had tapped into my creative juices and they were gushing and I began to accomplish things I had never believed I was capable of doing. I was drawing, writing my own poetry and composing music. I no longer wanted to play covers with the band; I wanted to record and perform original music. I saw many of the things I once took for granted in a new light. In my altered state I felt I had actually made contact with the spirit of the real God and became enlightened to the insanity of my religion. It was all kind of surreal and strange. I knew I was no longer the same person I was before I tripped, only in a good sense. At first, my band mates gave me a hard time, but after listening to a few of my compositions, we started to slowly incorporate originals into our sets, something I found to be much more fulfilling. For the next couple of years, as much as things stayed the same, in my mind, they were also quite different.

During the summer of '69, Jack, Jenny and Frank ventured up to Woodstock. Willy and I, only because we loved creature comforts such as a toilet and a clean bed, decided not to go. Jack returned from his three day excursion with energy, inspiration and high hopes for Electric Dust. By then, all of us had our driver's licenses and loved knowing we didn't have to depend upon others to get around.

September of 1969 began our last year at St. Stanislaw's. I no longer had any tolerance for Catholicism and what I felt were all of her superstitious, guilt-ridden lies, the sexually repressed men clad in dresses who posed as God's servants and the ridiculous rules and regulations coming from the gold and marble palace in Rome. Maybe the acid aided in raising my consciousness, I don't know for sure, but religion had certainly stopped making a drop of sense to me. I couldn't wait until graduation day.

We appeared in our last high school play in the spring of 1970. Mr. Mulroney told us he was going to hate to see us go because in all the years he'd been directing high school plays, he'd never seen attendances such as the ones he'd witnessed since we'd been involved. He was really a cool guy and I felt like we were abandoning him, but I lost my love for theatre and couldn't wait for it to all be over. Jenny had decided to quit drama in her senior year at Blessed Redeemer, making it a lot less enjoyable for Jack. He was in love with Jen and no longer

The Three Extras

interested in meeting new girls. Willy and I, however, were still unattached and had high hopes that maybe some fresh female faces would turn up for what would be our last performance. Although we all wanted out of drama, Jack, always wanting to do the right thing, convinced us we owed it to Mr. Mulroney and should do it one last time. We did. We always listened to Jack.

Jack, Willy and I were cast as three of Captain Hook's pirates in a production of *Peter Pan*. We weren't the least bit enamored with performing in plays anymore, in fact it became embarrassing, so we requested roles with very few speaking parts. We didn't want to have to exert our energies memorizing anything. I guess we suddenly felt we were too cool. The play was another huge success; we drew our usual attention and received our undeserved riotous applause. As it turned out, a couple of new girls from Blessed Redeemer joined the cast and crew. One girl who took a liking to me was Maria Borelli. She was also a senior and one of the costume designers. It just so happened because she was assigned to work on the pirates' costumes, we saw each other often. We would chit-chat a lot about music and discovered we had similar tastes. Maria had natural beauty; she had shoulder length, dark brown hair parted slightly to the left, wonder-filled wide hazel eyes and a shy, delicate smile. She didn't wear make-up and the scent of her perfume, for lack of a better word, was intoxicating. When we were in rehearsal, I used to look forward to seeing her on the set.

It was cast party time again and I only attended with the hope of seeing Maria. Much to my delight, she was there and no sooner than I stepped foot inside the door, she was at my side. Willy elbowed me to the ribs and said, "Well, it looks like you're gonna be busy tonight!" The cast celebrations didn't have the same allure for me as they did when I was an underclassman. I didn't know if it was due to the few times I dabbled with hallucinogens, but I couldn't relate to my classmates anymore. I wasn't interested in the things they spoke about, the music they listened to, or the religion they were part of. Jack was off in a corner with Jenny all night and Willy mingled about like a rock star in search of a groupie. I asked Maria if she cared to take a walk, to which she consented, and I promised Willy I wouldn't leave him without a ride home.

Maria and I walked hand in hand, up and down the streets of the quiet neighborhood. We talked about school, family, friends, the play and the band. She seemed so innocent, almost angelic, and the fact that all I could think about was getting her high and into her pants was driving me crazy with guilt. I wasn't quite sure if I succumbed to the tempter lurking in the dark side of my conscience or the testosterone coursing through my veins, or if they were even one and the same, but I took out the joint I had tucked away in my shirt pocket and made Maria a premeditated offer, "Would you care to smoke a joint with me?"

She seemed a little taken aback at first, but I sensed she also trusted me when she said, "Do you think we should, I've never smoked pot before, but I've always been curious to try it…"

"Oh, it's not a big deal," I assured her, "If you don't want to, I understand how you…"

"No," she quickly interrupted, "If ever I'm going to try it, why not now and why not with you?"

We walked along, brazenly passing the illegal cigarette back and forth until she began to laugh a nervous laughter, "Oh my God!" she tittered, "I must be stoned! I need to sit down!"

We were both a little too wasted to return right to the party, so at Maria's suggestion, we climbed into the backseat of my dad's '67 Chevy Impala, which he was gracious enough to let me borrow that evening. The familiar stimulating smell of her perfume, along with being high, made me want her more than I ever wanted anything. She placed her hand behind my neck, pulled my face towards hers and began to kiss me with no restraint. Before I knew it, our hands were enthusiastically wandering under each other's shirts and in each other's pants like kids with a one day pass to explore every attraction in Disney World. On her most welcome suggestion, we undressed each other as quickly as toddlers tearing the wrapping paper from Christmas presents, until our bare bodies were slipping and sliding all over the Impala's leather seats. Even in the cramped conditions of a backseat of a car, I was able to maneuver my way on top of her without once disengaging from her impassioned ongoing kiss. Her beautiful baby-wide eyes locked gazes with mine, and knowing what was about to happen, I asked, "Are you okay with this?"

Her arms tightened around me and she cried again, "Why not now and why not with you?"

I accomplished what I had set out to do. I was no longer a virgin and I assumed neither was she. When the euphoria subsided, and we were mindful of our whereabouts, naked in the backseat of my parents' car on a suburban street, we hurriedly retrieved our clothes and got dressed. We re-entered the party, which by that time was winding down, to find Willy looking bored out of his mind and a bit miffed. "Where the fuck did you disappear to?" he wondered out loud.

"You wouldn't believe me if I told you!" I replied.

Maria and I quickly kissed goodnight, then she left with the friends she had arrived with. Jack and Jen had split not long after the party began and Willy and I, who showed up together, left together. When he took his place in the passenger seat of my dad's car for the drive home, just like a bloodhound, he inhaled, looked at me funny, and in a scene right out of a Sherlock Holmes film, said, "I smell that chick's perfume! You had her in this car, didn't you?" I told Willy all the steamy details and he shrieked in jealous astonishment, "You screwed her in your dad's car? Get the fuck outta here."

"I told you, you wouldn't believe me!"

We said farewell to St. Stanislaw's on June 21st, 1970, Graduation Day. On that joyful morning, in an act of defiance, Jack, Willy and I let our hair hang down from under our green graduation caps, over our ears and collars, a symbol of our newfound freedom. No more hair spray, walking with outstretched necks, or hiding in stairwells. No more jackets and ties, no more Brothers, no more drama or religion. Before the ceremony, the three of us smoked a celebratory joint to help us endure the speeches, the presentation of awards, the singing of the school song and all the pomp and circumstance of the institution we despised. After receiving our diplomas, the class of '70 marched double file out the doors of the auditorium to the cheers of parents, relatives and friends. The three of us shed our gowns, flung our caps and never looked back.

The Three Extras

John Rullo

~EVERYTHING CHANGES~

I spent a good part of the summer of 1970 with Maria. Jennifer was acquainted with her from high school and during those months they became close. Jen liked the idea of having another female in the gang. Electric Dust was playing at The Courthouse regularly. Frank had an older cousin who managed a recording studio in Long Island City and let us record our original material during off-hours free of charge. That summer we were one big happy family. We spent July and August going to concerts, playing gigs, and getting stoned. When Maria and I weren't hanging out with the band, nothing could keep us apart…literally. We explored every inch of each other's body and had pretty incredible sex at every available opportunity; in the car, at the park, at the beach, in our garage, and even in her parent's laundry room. We were addicted to the pleasure of each other's company.

Willy, Jack, and I got accepted into Queens College, located less than a mile from St. Stanislaw's. The only reason we enrolled was to appease our parents. Our folks were all very aware of the fact we wanted to be rock stars, but warned us about the instability of show biz and advised us about the importance of having a back-up plan, which included a college degree. Jennifer and Frank didn't get accepted into Queens but registered at the local Community College, keeping our circle still intact.

It was near the end of August, however, when Maria dropped the bomb. Her parents weren't very fond of the idea of their only daughter spending all her time in the company of a psychedelic rock band; in fact, they heard us perform once and told her we were horrendous. God knows how they would have felt if they really knew what we were up to. Barely able to get the words out, she finally let me in on the bad news that she'd be going away to college. She got a free ride to a university in Ohio and her folks were resolute about her accepting the offer.

"I'll be home on holidays," she said softly and seeing I wasn't taking it too well, she caressed my cheek and gently continued, "I'll call you every night!"

"Yeah, Ohio's not too far," I said unconvincingly, "I could even take a drive on the weekends to visit..."

My heart ached with the hurt of knowing Maria would soon be gone. Although we only spent that one summer together, it was the best summer of my life, three months of Nirvana. The last night we were together, we were entwined in each others' arms, wishing and hoping for time to stand still. We couldn't pull our mouths apart, kissing madly as the salty taste of our tears reminded us that within the next twenty-four hours we'd be far apart. It was difficult trying to describe the emptiness I felt knowing it was just a matter of time before each of us would meet someone else. I knew she was never going to call me every night as much as I knew I wasn't going to drive to Ohio; I had no idea where Ohio even was!

Being students at a large city college was a far cry from the four years we spent at a strict, small private Catholic school. It was post-Woodstock and the country was involved in an ongoing war in Viet Nam. Nobody cared what we wore, what we looked like, what we believed in, or if we even showed up to class. It required a tremendous amount of discipline not to abuse the freedoms we were given. It was Jack who suggested we go to

Queens because it was close to home, it was free, and mostly because it wouldn't interfere with the life of the band. None of us had any idea about what course of study we should take, what major we should choose, or what we wanted to be when we grew up or if we even wanted to grow up. Our only interest was playing in a rock band. Queens College had a well-regarded music department, but to major in music meant having to learn all about music theory, classical, opera, jazz; in other words, it meant studying, something we desperately wanted to avoid. We were rockers, and we believed it was all about feel! I was writing and drawing abstract art, but I had no desire to confine my passions to the structure of a classroom. I was satisfied with my ability, and being the know-it-all teenager I was, didn't need a professor to teach me how to express myself any better than I thought I was already able to.

    Perusing the college catalog and the areas of study the school had to offer, Jack stumbled upon Communication Arts and Sciences and strongly recommended we give it a whirl. It seemed like we could take classes on the subjects of television, radio, and film with little or no effort and possibly have fun doing so. Course descriptions explained how students would be expected to take on projects in the field of entertainment, creating radio and television programs and producing films, something we were at least familiar with. There was no way I would have been able to suffer through math, science and history again. Jack, being the assertive, take-charge kind of guy he was, selected all our classes, planning it out so that the three of us had the very same schedules, enabling us to share rides, books, and homework assignments.

    I'd always loved going to the movies. I was continually dragging my friends to artsy Manhattan theatres to see what they

The Three Extras

considered "off the wall" foreign films. Each and every time they unenthusiastically sat through another one of my recommendations, Jenny would cry out, "Damn it John Colletti, this is the last time I go to the movies with you!" One evening we had all agreed to see *Easy Rider*, and after the film Jack had mentioned how we ought to make a movie of our own. College gave us that opportunity.

Professors Chuck Jones and Larry Roberts were frustrated Hollywood directors who settled for what they believed were slightly less rewarding careers teaching film production to young aspiring film makers. They were actually two pretty cool guys who were more interested in creativity, originality and imagination than they were with how well their students could memorize text book information. Just like it was in high school when Mr. Mulroney approached us to get involved in dramatics, for some strange reason both professors found the three of us interesting and often asked if we ever considered acting in front of a camera. They claimed although neither of them could put their finger on it, there was an aura about us they deemed as captivating and marketable. For a while we thought they might have been gay and patronized us with the intent to win our trust and affection, but we were dead wrong. As we got to know them, we realized we were imbeciles to even entertain those thoughts and that they really believed we had movie star qualities. As it turned out, they were right.

Jack had certainly put on us the right path. Most of our college courses were challenging, fun adventures. Many of the classes in which we were enrolled required our assignments be performed in groups, and one of the benefits about the three of us taking classes together was that from the day we stepped foot on campus, we were looked upon as a group; we always got to work with each other. Our first project was to produce a Super 8 film which implemented the use of various special effects achieved through the primitive techniques of splicing and in-camera editing. Jack, always the first to have an idea spring up in his head, suggested we make a space movie. We built a makeshift spaceship in my parents' garage, making use of any scrap metal and wood we could find. I dug out the Christmas lights from their attic and strategically placed them all around it. Disguising football helmets with window screen and aluminum foil, we designed our own uniquely original space helmets. By utilizing flexible clothes dryer hose and old sheets, we created space suits and were soon ready for lift-off.

    The plot of our first feature film involved Willy and me as two astronauts who travel through space to another planet. When we step down from our space vehicle, we discover that we landed in a prehistoric world where we are face to face with herds of angry dinosaurs. Rushing back up into our craft, we blast off, narrowly escaping our demise. The highlight of our film was a scene in which I attempted to mix a glass of Tang. After unscrewing the lid, I open the jar only to have the orange powder spill out all over the place. Because Jack was able to film the scene in slow motion and with Willy and me sitting in an upside down position, it appeared as though there was no gravity, causing the Tang to float upwards and out of the jar. Jack was a cinematographic genius! By splicing scenes from the 1950's monster movies we had purchased at an E. J. Korvette's department store together with the footage we shot in the garage of colored lights, strobe effects and close-up shots of our terror-filled faces, we created our very first masterpiece. When the final credits rolled after the class viewed our movie, they applauded wildly. The professors praised our work and we were each graded with an A plus; not too shabby for beginners.

The Three Extras

The band was still in full swing. Every so often, Jimmy from the Bee Hive would call. His club closed down because of the constant complaints from neighboring residents and a couple of drug busts, but he still had some connections with other venues and continued to get us gigs. We didn't make enough money to make it worth his while by offering him a commission, so we never understood why he would always been so willing to help us out. The Courthouse was still home base for us and one Friday night just before we were about to go on, Jennifer walked in with two girls we had never met before. She introduced them as Joanna and Tracy, new friends she had made in college. I had finally gotten over Maria and Willy was raring and ready to meet anyone, so both of our interests had perked.

Jenny took Willy and me aside and said, "You are going to love these girls. They are cool and so much fun to hang with!"

"Pretty cute too," Willy replied with approval.

Turning to me with gleaming eyes and a big smile on his face, Willy whispered, "I like Tracy, you could have Joanna," as if we had a choice or either one of them had any interest in us.

Truth be told, both girls were gorgeous, and for some reason, I just so happened to be more attracted to Joanna anyway, so Willy had nothing to worry about as far as competition from me. Joanna was around five foot six; she had waist-length mousy brown hair tied back in a loose braid. She was wearing low-cut, tight fitting, bell-bottom, faded-blue jeans with tattered edges and no back pockets, displaying a perfect behind. She was wearing a loose-fitting turquoise sweatshirt with the collar removed and a self-made slit extending down just a few inches from the neckline. Her high cheek bones, glossy full lips and wide sea-green eyes held me spellbound.

Tracy was equally beautiful. She was a few inches shorter, had a little darker complexion and shiny black hair that hung just past her petite shoulders, just brushing two very full breasts. Willy couldn't keep his eyes off of her.

Frank had met his sweetheart at school too. She was a Puerto Rican girl named Carmella who also showed up at The Courthouse on that same night to cheer us on. Frankie had to sneak around with Carmella because his parents were extremely prejudiced against any race that wasn't white. There was no chance of his ever introducing her to his parents. Their ignorance embarrassed him, but we loved her.

We were scheduled to play The Courthouse again on the following Saturday night so we didn't have any equipment to pack up. Jack suggested all eight of us head over to a diner for either a very late night snack or early morning breakfast. As usual, everyone agreed, and before long we were all sitting around a large table. The customary tokes on the post-gig joint put us all in a very jovial and hungry state. The new people among us commented on how much they loved the band while a waiter and two waitresses crammed our table with everything from cheeseburgers deluxe, onion rings and pickles, to waffles, French toast, scrambled eggs with bacon and chocolate shakes.

"I told you they were great!" Jenny reminded her two friends.

"Really cool," Joanna agreed, "Don't hear many bar bands play the stuff these guys do!"

Willy and I wanted so badly to make an impression upon Tracy and Joanna we ended up doing most of the talking. As we were filling the girls in on our history, it must have suddenly dawned on Jack that Frank was unusually quiet. Jack inconspicuously tapped me on the shoulder to steal my attention away from the new girls for a moment, and gestured for me to take notice of Frankie. "What's with him?" he asked. Frank had a distant gleam in his eyes, making it seem as if he were a million miles away and deep in thought.

I gave Willy a nudge and asked the very same question Jack did. Willy had accidentally dropped his napkin on the floor and reached down to pick it up. When he returned to his sitting position, the expression on his face was priceless. He was dying to let me on something, but at the same time, didn't want to draw too much attention to the situation, especially from our potential new girlfriends.

"Quick!" he ordered with a whisper, "Pretend like you dropped your fork, and then pick it up."

"What?" I asked curiously, "Why would I want to do that?"

"Shut up and just do it," he snapped authoritatively.

I followed Willy's orders and after seeing what I saw, choked while trying to control my laughter. Carmella had opened Frankie's fly, wrapped a napkin around his penis and was pleasuring him by hand right there under the table, which explained the blank faraway look on his face. Jack caught on, dropped his knife onto the floor and took a peek. Frank had no clue we knew what was going on and Carmella had no shame. The two of them didn't care who was present or where they were, they could never keep their hands off each other.

Joanna had taken the seat right beside me, and Tracy beside Willy, just as if it had been planned that way. I was so fixated on Joanna that by the time the check arrived, I was head over heels in love. Coincidentally, so was Willy. The following day, both Willy and I got a call from Jack notifying us that Jenny's friends had a great time and the feelings were mutual.

During our first three years at Queens, we were having the time of our lives. The band was getting quite a bit of press, making us out to be local rock stars and we even had label interest from ABC records. The four of us were settled with significant others. Willy paired up with Tracy, Joanna and I were going strong, and Carmella and Frank were still seeing each other in spite of his parents' disapproval. He just made it a point to keep her as far away from them as he could. Jack, Willy and I were doing great in school, making quite a name for ourselves among the faculty and students of the Communications Department. Willy and I owed our good grades to Jack who just kept coming up with one great idea after another. Not only were his ideas brilliant, he figured out how to execute them. Basically, Willy and I just went along with whatever Jack told us to do. We churned out radio programs, television shows, and commercials way beyond what any of our fellow classmates were able to produce. One Sunday afternoon, we had all gone to the movies to see *A Clockwork Orange* by Stanley Kubrick and Jack got the brainstorm we should submit a parody of the movie as our short film assignment. We assembled together members from our circle of friends and under Jack's direction, produced one gory bloodbath of a film. We had so many laughs and so much fun while trying to produce the most violent and gruesome film we could. We managed to churn out a couple of dismemberment scenes that even disturbed me. When some of the students actually had to look away when viewing it, we knew we did a great job. Our professor kept the film and used it as a model to inspire other students.

I had taken an elective course in screenplay writing. I don't know how and why the idea came to me, but I wrote a serious screenplay about a lesbian relationship where one of the partners got caught by her lover in an affair with a man. At that time, homosexuality was not as acceptable as it later became, so the story, along with the fact I could write it, made quite an impact on my professor. He had taken the screenplay to Professors Jones and Roberts with the idea of having us use it to make our first full blown production. I didn't know if it was because the script was so well written or because men are just fascinated by lesbians, but everybody was incredibly excited about shooting the movie.

    We had posted ads on several college bulletin boards in search of two actresses to be cast in the roles of the couple. We received numerous responses and auditioned at least twelve girls who claimed they would have no problem kissing and fondling in front of the camera under our amateur direction. The girls we eventually selected were very competent and extremely convincing in their parts. We were provided with the department's industry-caliber pro equipment which we used under the guidance of several members of past alumni. Jack, Willy and I shared the directing credits, although Jack called most of the shots. Willy billed himself as casting director solely because he convinced me to co-star as the male lover. Jack was a genius in the editing room and the final result was a film we were really quite proud of. When we viewed our tour de force for the class, they were blown away. The professors hailed us as cinematic boy wonders and they saw to it that the film was featured regularly at the college theatre. We became campus celebrities.

    Things took a turn for the worse during the first semester of our senior year at Queens. Electric Dust was scheduled to showcase at The Bitter End for the A&R staff of ABC Records and we were all pretty excited about it. One evening after arriving home from band practice, Frank and his parents got into a heated argument over his dating Carmella. According to Frank, his father gave him an ultimatum; "Break up with that spic, or get out of my house!" Frank had packed a suitcase and called to let each of us know he would be heading over to Carmella's house for a few days until either his father came to his senses or he could figure out his next move. Frankie never made it to Carmella's. As he was cruising along the Van Wyck Expressway on his way to her home in Jamaica, the front left tire of his 1963 Rambler blew out, he lost control of the vehicle, collided with a tractor trailer and was pronounced dead by the time the ambulance arrived. I remember getting two disturbing phone calls on that dreadful evening. The first one came from a troubled Carmella who had asked if I had heard from Frank. She said it was taking unusually long for Frank to arrive at her house and was wondering if maybe he had stopped by my place first. I told her not to panic, and mentioned that he probably stopped to get cigarettes or something. About ten minutes later, my mom called out my name with a sense of urgency, "Johnny," she hollered, "Pick up the phone; Jack needs to talk to you and he says it's an emergency..." I picked up the extension, and after he was certain my mom had hung up, he spoke in a tone so chilling, I knew what he was about to say would be devastating. "Johnny," he cried with a stutter, unable to disguise his anguish, "Frankie's dad just called me, man...Frank is dead; he was just killed in a car crash..." Stunned by the news, I sat motionless and listened as Jack tried unsuccessfully to hold back his tears. For just a moment I thought I had to be dreaming; things like this only happened in books and movies. Suddenly, unable to hold back any longer, Jack busted out in gut wrenching tears and I was overcome with waves of unrelenting nausea. My breathing became frightfully heavy and my parents came rushing into my room wondering what could possibly be the matter. I could barely get the words out of my trembling lips, "Frankie's dead..." and I sobbed uncontrollably. My folks tried their best to console me until Jack, Willy and the girls showed up at my door. We knew what we had to do and we knew not one of us could do it alone.

It was 11:45 pm when we all showed up at Carmella's. When she heard the car pull up, she came busting out of her front door like a stallion at the starting gate, her eyes overflowing with frightened tears. "Oh my God," she screamed, "What happened to Frankie?" Before we could say a word, she was on her knees crying hysterically as her mother and siblings watched from the window in confusion. Jenny knelt down beside her and pulled her close. There was nothing she could say. We all huddled around her and just by the sound of our sniffles and the look of our bloodshot eyes, Carmella knew.

Frankie's wake was without a doubt the saddest event I had ever attended. Mrs. Acuri had to be sedated in order to cope with the pointless death of her only child. Frank's dad blamed himself. While his trembling hands squeezed his ever-present white handkerchief, he begged for Carmella's forgiveness. Carmella, stone cold, spent every second of those agonizing days standing beside the coffin in silence, except for the sound of her unstoppable tears and periodic cries of, "Wake up Frankie, please wake up…." There were lines out the door of the funeral home with all the friends and fans of the band who had come to pay their respects. For some reason, it just wasn't quite sinking in for me. It was all very surreal. Joanna was at my side for the entire three day ordeal and I don't believe we even spoke two words to each other. I tried to convince myself I was having a very bad dream, knowing that if I wasn't, life was certainly not going to be the same. It wasn't.

It was painfully evident to Willy, Jack and me, that without Frank, Electric Dust could no longer continue. The showcase with ABC was indefinitely postponed, and all our pending gigs were cancelled. Carmella eventually stopped communicating with any of us because she said it was too painful; we only made her think of Frank. Like three lost souls with no inspiration or desire to continue with anything, we took a short break from life, cutting at least two weeks of classes.

The pain of not having Frank around eventually subsided enough for us to get back to our lives and business as usual. Maybe we had been feeling a little too sorry for ourselves with the demise of the band, but taking the advice of our concerned parents we returned to school and tried our best to settle in to the swing of things. One afternoon, during the winter of '73, I was surprised to see Jenny sitting by herself on the front steps of my house. When she saw my car pull up, she immediately dashed towards me. "John," she called out fretfully, "I need to talk to you!" It looked as if she might have been crying.

"What's wrong, Jennifer?"

"I don't know what I'm going to do," she said as she paced nervously, "How can I tell Jack after all that just happened?"

"Tell him what?" I pried.

"I'm pregnant, John Colletti, I'm fuckin' pregnant!"

Jenny's words sent me for a loop. I just couldn't understand how a guy like Jack could get himself into such a predicament. He was so methodical, so careful and so calculated in almost everything he did, I assumed that even in the heat of passion, he would have had things in control.

"Relax, Jenny," I said softly and sympathetically, trying to calm her down, "You're going to have to tell him because he's going to find out eventually!"

"I know," she stammered, "I know, unless I…"

The Three Extras

"Don't even think about it," I cut in, knowing she was alluding to ending the pregnancy before he could find out, "Just tell him; he'll understand."

Jennifer broke the news to Jack later that same evening. Initially, he felt as if the weight of the world had just fallen upon his shoulders, wondering what else could possibly go wrong. Although getting married and having children was something they eventually planned on, the timing was wrong. Jack still hadn't completed school or given a thought to working a straight job. He told Jenny not to worry and to give him a day or two to come up with a solution. The very next morning, he asked Jennifer to marry him. When Jack made his mind up about something, there was no stopping him. He met with Jennifer's parents, took complete responsibility for the situation and asked for her hand in marriage. He told them he had a plan. He was going to get a full time job, complete his schooling at night and find an apartment. Jennifer's folks were pretty cool and fortunately very well off. Admiring Jack for his honesty and integrity, they offered to help him and their daughter in any way they could. All involved wanted to keep Jenny's pregnancy under wraps, so the arrangement was to have a wedding before she showed any signs of a baby within. Everything fell into place rather quickly. Jen's dad was a bigwig at Macy's and managed to fit Jack into a well-paying position with the company. He also fronted whatever money they needed to secure them a place to live. On March 2nd, 1974, Jack and Jennifer became husband and wife. They were the first of my friends to tie the knot. The ceremony took place at Jenny's church, followed by a simple affair at an elegant neighborhood catering facility, The Terrace. Jack's brother Eddie was his best man, Willy and I were ushers, and Tracy and Joanna were Jenny's bridesmaids. It was the newlyweds' wishes not to make the affair too extravagant or to place a financial burden on any of their friends, so everyone, including the wedding party, was asked to dress casually. They hired "The Banshees," a great cover band we had once heard in a neighborhood bar, and during the reception, Willy, Jack and I had the opportunity to sit in with them for a song or two. It was the first time we played together since Frankie died and probably the last time Jack ever picked up his bass.

It was kind of exciting having friends who had their very own place. The Reilly's rented a quaint second floor garden apartment in Bayside, Queens with a beautiful view of the park. The six of us would hang out there on weekends where we watched movies, listened to records and observed Jenny's stomach grow larger and larger by the week. It seemed so out of character for Jack to have a clean shaven face, a conventional haircut and corporate job. A man of his word, he kept his promise to Jen and her family, joined the nine to five world and completed his college degree by attending night classes.

Queens College just wasn't the same for Willy and me without the security of having Jack around to do the thinking for us. Going to class became drudgery and with only months to go before earning his degree, Willy dropped out. I tried to convince him to do otherwise and stick it out until graduation, but having a glimpse of how wonderful he perceived married life would be, he was determined to follow in Jack and Jen's footsteps by marrying Tracy.

Slowly but surely, everything was changing in our lives. In early November of '74, Jenny gave birth to a seven pound, nine ounce baby girl. They named her Lorraine, and Jack was the proudest Dad anyone could ever imagine. Once they became parents, Jack and Jenny's love nest was no longer our weekend hangout. Unless we had an invite or we made plans to go out well in advance, we saw less and less of them. In the meantime, Willy contacted his Uncle Eugene, who was a union delegate for the railroad. Having heard many great things about a career backed by a union, such as, good pay, great benefits and a retirement package with a pension, Willy had approached him with the hopes of being able to land a position with the Long Island Railroad. I couldn't believe my two closest friends, the guys with whom I shared big dreams, had sold out and were thinking about things like medical benefits and retirement packages. Within a week after he inquired, Willy's uncle succeeded in hooking up his nephew with a secure job as a ticket taker for the LIRR, complete with navy blue uniform and dorky conductor's cap. After graduating Community College, Tracy enrolled in a vocational school where she trained to be a dental assistant and was able to obtain a respectable job in a local office immediately after receiving her certification. Together, Willy and Tracy were making a decent amount of money, and following the advice of Tracy's dad, put a small down payment on a cute little house in Merrick, Long Island. Joanna and I spent many a weekend trekking out to Nassau County to help Willy and Tracy paint and decorate what was soon to become their new home.

    On Sunday March 9th 1975, a week after Jack and Jenny's first anniversary, Willy and Tracy vowed before a packed church to love and honor each other until death do them part. Jack, Jenny, Joanna and I, proudly decked out in our tuxedos and gowns, were the only ushers and bridesmaids. Not wanting to choose between Jack and me, Willy asked his older brother to be his best man and to keep her parents happy, Tracy chose her older cousin as her matron of honor. The reception was held at DaVinci's, one of the nicest catering facilities in the area, and it must have set Tracy's folks back quite a bit. To me, it seemed like they spared no expense. It was the first conventional wedding any of us had ever attended, complete with seven piece house band, cocktail hour and a menu with three main courses to choose from. Everybody appeared to have had a great time, even though every half hour or so, Jenny and Jack kept taking turns running out to the phone booth in the lobby to check up on the babysitter. As delighted as I was for my friends, I was feeling a bit melancholy. At one time, we would have never passed up an opportunity to sit in with a band. At Willy and Tracy's wedding, it had never occurred to anyone to ask us to play and it never even occurred to us to offer. I was starting to fear we had surrendered to the system we had worked so hard to escape. Were we getting old before our time?

Feeling somewhat abandoned by the pair I had been inseparable from for the past ten years, I knew I had better start making some decisions. Somehow, I had managed to tolerate school without the presence of my comrades, sucking it up until the end and finally getting my bachelors degree. I had been working part-time at a local music store, giving guitar lessons and selling equipment. After completing school, I still had no idea of what I wanted to do, so I accepted my boss's offer to work at the store full time. I had always counted on the band making it, and I guess I just never wanted to face the reality it was over. I tried putting together other bands, joined a few, but nothing had the magic, the fun, or the unique sound of Electric Dust.

Joanna was pretty cool about not pressuring me to get married. I knew after seeing her two closest friends settle down, she had to be wondering if a wedding was going to happen anytime in her near future. She was working as a receptionist for a busy law firm in Mineola, and taking some night classes with the hopes of one day becoming a teacher. She would tell me time and time again about the many people who would stop by her desk curiously asking as to why she never sought after a career in modeling. The truth is I used to ask her the same. Joanna was uniquely beautiful but somehow I sensed she was strangely insecure about her looks and her abilities, which may be why she settled for a character like me. I often tried to figure out why she lacked confidence, but as I got to know her parents, I deduced it was partially due to their inability to offer any signs of encouragement and affection. Unbending staunch Catholics, they were kind of flakey and extremely distant and my attempts at getting close to them always failed. I wouldn't say her folks were malicious or uncaring, I seriously believed they just didn't know any better and because of their incapacity, Joanna quickly learned how to succeed on her own even with the handicap of having low self esteem. Somehow, this aspect of her personality made me want to nurture and care for her.

On Christmas Day 1975, I found myself willingly surrendering to tradition by giving Joanna a modest engagement ring and telling her I wanted to get married. I wasn't a big fan of ritual and tradition, but I realized this wasn't all about me. Joanna was overjoyed, and on Sunday, the sixth of June, 1976, it was our turn to march down the aisle and join the ranks of married couples. Besides being uninvolved in our lives, Joanna's parents were not well-to-do by any stretch of the imagination, and even if they wanted to, could not afford to throw us a wedding as elaborate as Willy and Tracy's. My folks had offered to contribute, so among all of us, we managed to put together a nice party, even though there was a good deal of compromising involved. To keep all the parents happy I agreed to a Catholic Church service if everyone else agreed to a casual outdoor affair. We reached an agreement. My dad had a close business associate who was a silent partner in a restaurant with park-like grounds in the Village of Roslyn on the north shore of Long Island. He made us an offer we couldn't refuse which allowed me to get my way as far as the reception taking place outdoors. Again, we broke the rules; I had two best men, Jack and Willy; and Joanna had two maids of honor, Tracy and Jennifer. There were no ushers and no bridesmaids; we just couldn't see putting everyone through the trouble or the expense. The weather couldn't have been better; there wasn't a cloud in the sky or a drop of humidity in the air. The sunshine was plentiful, the temperature reached a high of 76 degrees and everyone, including Joanna's mom and dad, seemed to have enjoyed themselves immensely. For the first time in a while, things seemed to be looking up.

    Like anything else in life, being married took some getting used to. I was no longer responsible only for myself. I had to take Joanna into account for everything I did or planned on doing or not doing. Joanna had mentioned to me on more than one occasion she wanted to have a family. At the time, we were living in a three-room apartment not far from Jack and Jenny's. I realized my job at the music store wasn't going to afford me the necessary foundation for providing for a family. I also realized, once she became a mother, I would want Joanna to be at home with the baby and not have to worry about going to work. I had to cast aside any notions I had about not conforming to society and put my energies towards seeking out better employment. Once again, Jack helped out by informing me his sister-in-law, Karen, Eddie's wife, had just taken a position in the Human Resources department with the phone company. When recommending I should give her a call, his creative mind never at rest, he said, "I've got this great idea, John, maybe you can suggest it to them when you get the job!"

    "What now Jack? You never stop thinking, do you?"

"How about this," he proposed, "A gadget you could hook up to your phone that will enable you to see the number of the party calling...This way if you don't want to talk to them, you don't have to answer the phone; something on the order of a caller identification system!"

"Brilliant!" I exclaimed, "You think we'll ever see something like that in our lifetime?"

"Hey, after you convince GM about my idea of starting a car by remote control, you need to work on Ma Bell about caller recognition and I'll split my millions with you!"

We both laughed, almost believing Jack's ideas were feasible.

Karen was incredibly helpful by setting me up with an interview. Within two weeks I received the call to report for training. As far as jobs go, it was decent enough for a guy like me who didn't want to wear a jacket and tie or be cooped up in an office for forty hours a week. I was always on the road and in a different place every day. I didn't have to cut my hair or adhere to any dress code. The job paid well, offered great benefits and a pension, but it was the furthest thing from rock stardom. When I checked in for work on that first day, I remember feeling like I had succumbed. From the moment I first slipped my timecard under the clock to punch in, I anxiously awaited the day I'd be punching out for the very last time. As much as I loved Joanna, I felt as if I had lost my identity, blending namelessly into the masses, joining the rat race to nowhere.

As the years inconspicuously galloped along, life took Jack, Willy, and me in different directions. Jack's position at Macy's became more and more demanding, requiring him to make frequent trips to Europe and Asia. He and Jenny had two more children, boys, and moved to a pleasant community of

Long Island called Floral Park, where they bought an oversized cape on a quiet street of cookie cutter houses. When Jack wasn't traveling, he dedicated his time and energies to Little League Baseball, coaching both his sons until they left for college.

Willy worked hard at the LIRR making himself invaluable by covering any shift on any line. Eventually someone took notice of his reliability and offered him a supervisory position. Willy and Tracy had two children, both girls. They were happy in the house they had lived in since they were married. Instead of moving into a larger home, they upgraded by doing some improvements, added an extension and remained there until both daughters were married.

Joanna and I took the natural path of most apartment dwellers from Queens and also migrated to Long Island. When Joanna became pregnant with our first child in 1981, we knew we had to move to larger quarters and so we bought a three bedroom colonial in Wantagh, just a couple of towns away from Willy. Three years after the birth of our daughter, Joanna gave birth to twin boys. Running out for disposable diapers, mowing the lawn, helping with the laundry, and dozing off on the couch, helped in making life turn out to be a far cry from the exciting career in show biz life I had once envisioned.

Because of our hectic schedules, between working long hours and raising families, Jack, Willy, the girls and I rarely got the opportunity to socialize. No matter how many times we had called each other trying to make arrangements to get together, it hardly ever seemed to work out. On the few occasions when our calendars surprisingly aligned, we had magical times laughing and recalling the good old days, realizing that the threads of our memories would hold us together forever.

None of us, however, had ever missed any of the others' special events. Whether it was the birth and the weddings of our children, the passing away of our parents, or the special celebrations of life, we were always there for each other. Like now.

~INTERMISSION~

    I couldn't believe I was still awake. Reminiscences of the life and times of the three of us were flashing before me, one scene after another, bringing a smile to my face one second and tears to my eyes the next. I wondered what ever had happened to all those who appeared in the screenplay of my life and whether or not I have co-starred in any of their life stories. In what turned out to be a brief intermission, I got up to relieve my bladder. What broke through the memories may have been all the coffee I drank earlier at Lorraine's. I stumbled to the bathroom, and then slowly hobbled back into bed. Still, I did not sleep. My peek into the past continued.

The Three Extras

John Rullo

~WHEN DID THIS HAPPEN? ~

~When I was a boy, my dad used to tell me to treasure every minute because one's lifetime is like the blink of an eye. "It goes fast, son," he warned, "It seems like only minutes ago when I was your age thinking I had life by the balls...." His words rang true; I blinked and thirty years were suddenly gone. My three kids were grown and on their own; two were married, one still looking for Mrs. Right. For a while, we three compadres and our wives were seeing a lot of each other just by attending the weddings of our kids. We were all different, but of the six of us, Jack had changed the most. Between the demands of his job, the repeated traveling overseas, and his involvement in his town, he neglected his health. He was always eating on the run, a diet consisting mostly of fast food. Eventually, an excess of pizza, French fries and diet-Coke will take anybody down. Jack gained some weight and lost some hair; no longer looking like the Rock God he was a couple of decades ago. Willy and I managed somehow to stay in shape. We still had full heads of hair, although the silver signs of aging started to appear like dandelion on a beautiful green lawn. For women in their mid-fifties who worked and bore children, Joanna, Jennifer and Tracy still looked wonderful, miraculously holding onto their youthful beauty. Naturally we all had some creases and laugh lines here and there, but for the most part, we held up.

The world had certainly changed since our high school days. Advancements in technology were staggering. Now and then I would wonder if humans were progressing so rapidly due to the intervening of alien life forms. How did all the new technology just so happen to develop in leaps and bounds in such a short time frame? So many of the ideas Jack had dreamed up almost thirty years ago came to fruition; Caller ID, remote control start, and music video channels became a part of every household. If we had only known how to develop those brainstorms of his, we could have been billionaires! No sooner was a new gadget introduced that it became obsolete. We converted from an analog world into a digital one. The thousands of record albums I had collected through the years and had stored upon rows and rows of shelves, taking up several square feet of wall space, could all be reduced to a microscopic chip. The planet seemed to get smaller and smaller and less cluttered with wires as wireless communication devices such as cell phones, I-pods, I-pads and like gadgets became permanent fixtures on everyone. One day Jack had asked me about it, "John," he wondered, "Could you imagine what we could have accomplished if we had computers and the Internet when we went to school?" It was scary to think of all the amazing possibilities.

In the summer of 2008, I was the first of my friends to retire. The time between the first day I punched in and the last day I punched out seemed like a blur. So much seemed to have happened and yet, nothing had happened. Many of us fail to take notice of things and events as they are occur, but then ten or twenty years down the road we look back in wonder at all the monumental changes that took place right before our eyes. Kids mature, parents pass away, we grow old, the cost of living escalates, technology improves, attitudes change, and strong held beliefs weaken.

I was ecstatic over not having to set an alarm clock and be rushing out the door every morning to get to work on time. Retirement was something I knew I could get accustomed to very easily. It was on a Tuesday afternoon in July. I was sitting out on my deck sipping an ice cold beer when the phone rang and the Caller ID ironically flashed the name Jack Reilly above his number. It was very out of the ordinary for Jack or Jenny to be calling on a weekday afternoon. I answered the phone to somber tone of Jenny's voice. "Hi John," she faintly spoke, "I have bad news…"

"What happened?" I cried out and quickly jumped to attention like a soldier in the presence of a drill sergeant.

"Jack's in St. Francis Hospital; last night he had a heart attack," she announced worriedly, "It was so fuckin' scary, John!

"You're kidding?" I blurted out in a shocking moment of disbelief, "Is he okay?"

"Right now, he's stable," she said, "Doctors have to do some further tests…."

Immediately, I hopped into the car and headed to St. Francis. When I arrived, his brother Eddie was at his bedside. Jack's eyes were shut and he was all wired up to blinking and beeping monitors, tubes went into to his veins and IV bags were hanging down around him like Christmas ornaments. Eddie had aged quite a bit since I had seen him last, looking more like Jack's dad than his brother. He gave me a nod, shook my hand and filled me in on his younger brother's condition. The doctors had placed two stents in Jack's arteries and implanted a pacemaker. Jack's eyes slowly opened when he heard my voice. He looked over at me and then toughed out a smile that plainly stated, "How the hell did this happen to me?" I grabbed his hand, gave it a gentle squeeze and assured him he was going to be alright.

"Were you that envious you had to go to these extremes to get out of work?" I joked, resulting in a tenuous smile from my friend.

"Johnny," Jack called out just above a whisper, "I've got a great idea!"

"What is it, Jack?" I asked to humor him.

"We need to come up with a device whereby the human eye serves as a lens and records the events of the day. The information gets stored in chip and can then be uploaded to a computer and transferred to a DVD for viewing, eliminating the need for cameras! What do you think?"

Eddie looked at me and grinned, "He's nuts!"

"All geniuses are nuts!" I told him, "Hey, thirty years ago he dreamed the idea of Caller ID and I thought he was nuts!"

Jack smiled, directing his reply to both of us, "I'm telling you, one day there will be no more cameras!"

"Have I ever doubted you, my friend?"

Jack took a labored deep breath and then let me in on yet another one of his brainstorms. "Johnny, we need to invent a dream catcher!"

"They already have dream catchers," I informed him, "My daughter used to have one hanging in her bedroom…"

"No!" he corrected me, "Not those stupid things, I'm talking about a gadget that could be wired up to somebody's head while they're asleep and actually record the images of their dreams so they could get to view them the next day…You know how we all forget our dreams! How great would that be if we could store our dreams…?"

"I think you need to get some rest," Eddie eagerly suggested.

Jack's head sunk back down into his pillow, his overactive imagination shifted into rest mode and he drifted off to sleep.

Two months after Jack was released from the hospital, he was back up on his feet and gradually getting back to near-normal. Even though he put himself on a regimented diet and exercise program, his doctor told him returning to work was out of the question. Jack was always thinking ahead, so he was wise enough to have put money aside in case of emergency situations such as the one he was facing. He applied for social security disability and was approved. His lifestyle, however, had to change considerably. Although he was pleased about not having to travel abroad and commute to Manhattan every day, Jack was not one for sitting around with his ass glued to a couch and his eyes fixated on the television. As his health improved, it was only a matter of time before he came up with something that would keep him occupied.

Willy, in the meantime, was uncertain about retiring. He had put in more than enough time and had enough socked away in a retirement fund to live comfortably, but in the back of his mind lurked the fear something might go wrong. "Let's see what happens in six months," he would say. Six months later he would repeat himself, "Let's see what happens in six months!" Routine seemed to be a necessary part of Willy's life; it offset his insecurity.

I was keeping myself busy. I started playing around with the guitar again and entertained thoughts of putting together a cover band. My creative juices were flowing and I began working on a couple of ideas I had for novels. As far as I was concerned, twenty-five years of submitting to the structure of the working world was just a temporary setback. Joanna was working part-time and we tried as best as we could to stay out of each others' hair. It's crazy what happens to husbands and wives after being together for so many years. Just like all the other married couples we knew, we were taking each other for granted and our relationship was stagnating. I needed something more to fulfill me. I hated facing the fact I was already in my fifties and had no prospects of anything artistically promising in sight. The trouble with me was, as much as I considered myself a creative individual, all my past endeavors included the support of my two best friends. I never had what it took to go it alone.

On the morning of my 57th birthday, I received a call from Jack that changed my life.

"Johnny," he sang out cheerfully and positive, "How would you like to be in the movies?"

"What are you thinking of seeing?" I asked.

"I said, 'be in the movies' not 'go to the movies,'" he laughed.

"What the hell are you talking about; do I want to be in the movies?"

"I was just reading this article in Newsday about becoming a movie extra. The studios need them and the pay is pretty good. What do you say we look into it?"

"Sounds good to me," I said, humoring him in my usual way, "Let's check it out," all too aware that "we" meant "me." Jack was full of great ideas but always left it up to me to follow through, which was probably why nothing ever came of any of them. Success was always a united effort.

That same day, Tracy had called to wish me a happy birthday and I told her about the call I got from Jack.

"Johnny!" she shrieked, "That's crazy! One of our patients is a casting director, she was just in the office yesterday and we were talking about that very same article!"

"Do me a favor, Tracy...next time you see her, ask what it takes to be an extra in a movie."

"She's due back next week for a cleaning; I definitely will," she said, assuring me she would inquire.

Tracy kept her word and two weeks later, Jack, Willy and I were sitting side by side on a Manhattan bound train on our way to the office of Wendy Levine, talent coordinator at the Starlight Agency. Whenever the three of us were together, in spite of how we've aged, we felt the same spunk and charm of those three rebellious teenage boys whose energies merged in Room 107 all those years ago. As we would soon discover, others could feel it too. Ms. Levine's secretary instructed us to take a seat and in a nasally whine said, "Ms. Levine will see you shortly." Her office was located in a newly renovated building on 57th Street just off Broadway on the 23rd floor. Movie posters and photos of celebrities hung on the walls as if to tout the agency's success. The three of us sat there taking in the surrounding sights, including the panoramic view of the city from the oversized windows, anticipating what the outcome of our meeting would be. The secretary picked up her phone after three quick rings, then gently placed it down before calling our names, "Ms. Levine will see you now." She rose from her desk and led us down a lavishly decorated hallway to Wendy Levine's luxurious office.

"Good afternoon, gentlemen, Wendy, Wendy Levine! Which one of you handsome fellows is Tracy's husband?"

Willy stepped forward, extended his hand and introduced himself. "Pleased to meet you Wendy; I'm Willy, Willy Taylor. These are my good friends, Jack Reilly and John Colletti."

The Three Extras

Wendy greeted each of us with a handshake, feminine, yet firm. "Tracy is such a darling, I absolutely love her," she said, directing the compliment towards Willy, then eyeing up the three of us as if we were a single entity, she continued, "So, you want to be movie extras!"

Wendy looked nothing like I had expected her. For some reason, I pictured a glamorous, lanky blond with a knockout figure sporting stylish expensive clothing. Wendy was petite, with a body lacking curves. Her thick black hair was cut short exposing a few wiry gray strands. It looked as if she applied her make-up while sitting in the back seat of a cab that didn't miss a pothole. She was wearing an ordinary black pants suit and her perfect teeth and beautiful white smile paid homage to the dental skills of Tracy's boss.

"Sure," Jack replied enthusiastically, "Who wouldn't want to be in a movie?"

"I have to say," Wendy commented with an optimistic gleam in her eye, "The three of you men have an interesting look. You have an aura about you that I just can't put my finger on, but I have a hunch will be very marketable...."

In my best Robert DeNiro voice, which wasn't very good, I attempted to bring a little levity to the room and quoted the famous line from *Taxi Driver*, "You talking to me? Are you talking to me?"

Wendy picked up on my lousy impression and said, "No, I'm not talking to you, I'm taking to all three of you. Call me insane, but I see the three of you as a package. Give me a few days to make some calls. In the meantime, fill out this paperwork and these release forms. Maybe I'm crazy, but I'm getting very positive vibrations. Twenty-three years in the business and I've learned to follow my gut, and my gut is telling me that you guys have something. Remember, not everybody is camera friendly!"

"See that, we have something, we're camera friendly!" Jack said, his eyes lit up with excitement.

"Easy, Jack!" Willy warned, "Don't need you getting another heart attack!"

Wendy instructed us to follow her out of her office to a large room at the far end of a long corridor. We entered a photo studio, complete with backdrops, lighting, tripods and cameras. She introduced us to an eccentric looking fellow named Peter and his assistant, an intriguingly pretty young lady whose name was Elena. Peter was the skinniest man I had ever seen. His triple pleated black slacks were bunched up around his pencil-thin waistline, held up by a tightly pulled belt that had extended around him almost twice. His white shirt with the rolled up sleeves hung on him like a bed sheet, matching the color of his pasty skin, it appeared as if he'd never been exposed to sunlight! He wore his limp black hair tied back in a ponytail keeping it snug and in place by at least a dozen evenly positioned rubber bands.

Elena was a strikingly beautiful redhead, with short choppy hair, crystal blue eyes, and plump ruby lips. She was wearing a white lab coat and black canvas slip-on sneakers. She sized us up the second we were introduced, already planning her strategies.

"Elena is our make-up artist," Wendy announced, as if we couldn't tell, "She's the one responsible for making everyone look their absolute finest for the camera. Peter will be taking the photos we are going to need for your portfolio. He's by far one of the best in the business."

Rapidly blinking his eyes, Peter pretended not to be listening to the compliments as he tinkered with the settings on a camera while Elena signaled for us to take seats in front of a large brightly lit mirror.

"I'm going to leave you in their capable hands," Wendy pronounced as she hurriedly made her exit, "Be sure to stop back in my office before you leave."

Elena carefully studied our faces; dipping, dabbing, wiping, rubbing, combing, spraying and adding just the right touch of cosmetic magic to make us camera-ready. Willy, looking at himself in the mirror and feeling a little silly over the way he was being pampered, exclaimed, "I feel like a movie star already!" as his eyes, which were glued to Elena's stunning face, revealed his lecherous thoughts. No sooner did she apply her finishing touches to our middle-aged mugs, we were standing in front of a full length back drop, squinting from the arsenal of lights shining on us. Peter paced from side to side holding his light meter inches from each of our heads ensuring the perfection of every shot at every angle. For at least an hour the three of us posed as Peter shot away, trying his darnedest to make us relax, smile, be serious, be silly and look marketable.

After Peter called out, "That's a wrap!" we meandered back to Wendy's office where we were greeted by her secretary who directed us to go right in. Wendy was on the phone and motioned for us to take a seat on the couch across from her desk. As we patiently sat and waited, Jack's fingers were tapping against his knees; Willy was playing with his cell phone; and I stared out at the skyscrapers thinking about how, once again, I was in a situation all because of one of Jack's brainstorms.

We could hear Wendy finishing her conversation, "You won't be disappointed Sid, I think these three gentlemen are just what you've been looking for…That's perfect…I expect to hear from you by Friday…Good-bye, same to you." Wendy hung up the phone, stood up from behind her cluttered desk, looked at our hopeful faces and gave us the news, "Gents, I believe I may have lined up your first assignment; I'll have a definite on Friday. Until then, I'm going to need a name to identify your portfolio...uh, let me see, how about The Three Extras?"

"The Three Extras," Jack repeated, "I like the sound of that!"

As I sat sandwiched between Jack and Willy on an overcrowded rush hour train back to Long Island, my imagination was working overtime as fantasies of stardom swirled about in my head. My two friends were sitting quietly beside me so I could only assume they were entertaining the same ambitious thoughts.

At 12:02 on that following Friday, Wendy Levine called. Sid, the casting director she'd spoken to on the phone, went wild with enthusiasm when he saw our photos and instructed her to have us report to Citifield in Flushing a week from the following Monday to be cast as fans in the filming of a Master Card commercial. Willy still hadn't made the decision to retire, feeling insecure about being able to live on a pension, but he told us if he absolutely had to, he would call in sick on the day of the shoot.

"You'd better call in sick," I shouted, "Remember; it's all of us or none of us!"

"I shouldn't have a problem," Willy answered unconvincingly.

"You shouldn't have a problem?" I barked, "You better not fuck this up for us!"

"Don't worry, don't worry, I'll be there!"

"Why the heck don't you pack it in, Willy?" Jack asked, "This could be a whole new career for us!"

"I'll believe it when I see it!"

The Three Extras

Monday rolled around pretty quickly, and the three of us reported to the stadium as instructed. There were quite a few people on hand, many who had been hired only as seat-fillers. Our orders were to go directly to the Sky Club and not to get lost in the crowd. We found our way past the lines and arrived right on time. A rather muscular, bearded fellow, wearing sunglasses and a black silk director's jacket, looking more like a bouncer than a filmmaker, met us at the door, "You guys must be Wendy Levine's Three Extras!"

"That's us!" Jack verified proudly.

"You guys are going to work out perfectly, you've got just the look I've had in mind…Hi, my name is Sid Green, and I am the casting director for the shoot. Let me introduce you to Phil Spagnoli, he'll be directing and telling you guys essentially what to do."

We followed Sid over to the bar where he presented us to his colleague. "Phil, I'd like you to meet The Three Extras!"

"Nice to meet you," Phil said pleasantly, "These fellows are perfect, Sid; where did you find 'em?"

Sid proceeded to tell Phil all about the eager phone call he got from Wendy describing our "charming presence." "I'm telling you, Phil, Levine knows a face when she sees one and she just found us three!"

Phil was a handsome man, appearing to be in his 40's, but looked as if he were back in the 70's. His dark brown hair was long and combed straight back, just touching the collar of the same style silk jacket worn by Sid. Phil's neatly groomed sideburns extended below his ear lobes giving him that "Elvis" look. His brown eyes were clear and sparkling and the shape of his mouth seemed to be that of a permanent smile revealing perfectly straight day-glow teeth.

For a few minutes we were feeling a little unsure of ourselves, like we might have been the butt of a practical joke. It was illogical, almost dreamlike, how the three of us were getting so much attention and admiration for what we considered our rather average looks. Those suspicions quickly disappeared, however, when Phil let out with an enthusiastic, "What do you say we get to work!" Before we knew it, Jack, Willy and I were surrounded by a make-up crew and sitting in seats behind the third base dugout. As the cameras rolled, all we had to do was laugh, smile, give each other high-fives, and pretend to eat hot dogs, drink beer, eat peanuts and pay for our purchases with a Master Card. It was a long day of re-shooting the same scenes over and over again, but the weather was fabulous, we were given anything we wanted to eat or drink and supposedly, we were to get paid pretty well.

Within two weeks, a substantial check arrived in the mail for the "work" I performed on the Master Card shoot. "Wow!" I thought to myself, "A few of these babies every year and we'll be doing okay!" Willy called me that same day as excited as can be over the amount of money he made for doing such easy work. "If I could be certain to get one of these every once in a while," he admitted, "I'd retire yesterday!"

It wasn't until about a month after we had filmed the commercial that we each received a call from Wendy. "Be sure to watch channels 2, 4 and 7 tomorrow night between 8 and 11pm," she said with vibrant enthusiasm, "They're supposed to be airing your commercial. By the way, Sid and Phil were absolutely thrilled with you guys; expect another call soon!"

The following evening, we all gathered together at Willy and Tracy's house for a celebratory dinner and our first glimpse of our smiling faces on national TV. At approximately 8:30 that evening, Jenny let out a howling scream, "Oh my God! It's you!

How great is this!" as the six of us witnessed the screening of The Three Extras first commercial. Willy had set the DVR and if we replayed it once, we replayed it a thousand times. It was quite the thrill to see ourselves on television, especially looking as good as we did. Wendy was right; we did have an aura about us. We certainly gave a perfect impression of three personable, fun-loving, sexy, charming and successful middle-aged fellows.

"I have to admit," Joanna reluctantly admitted, "You guys look great on TV!"

"What do you mean, 'on TV'?" I quipped.

"You know what I mean," she said, trying to redeem herself.

It was an extremely memorable moment as the three of us basked in the glory of what we hoped would become our new career. Our phones rang continually with calls from family and friends who had seen us on television that evening. Among the slew of calls was a congratulatory one from Wendy who assured us this was just the beginning. They say it's all about "who you know," or "being in the right place at the right time." Little did we realize that somewhere in the universe, we found our right place and the wheels were turning in our favor!

In June of 2010, some of the alumni of St. Stanislaw had organized a forty year high school reunion. Jack, Willy and I had sworn for as long as we lived, we'd never step foot back into that school again, unless, of course, we became rock stars. Being in a nationally televised commercial was close enough, so we all decided to attend.

It was a strange feeling to be walking down the oddly familiar corridors where we spent four years of our young lives ducking the dean. The celebration took place in the gymnasium and the turnout was surprisingly large. Sadly, many of the faces were hardly recognizable, and if it weren't for the name tags pinned to everyone's shirt, I would have been clueless. Time wasn't very kind to some of our old classmates. Joanna, Jenny and Tracy looked like Maxim models compared to some of the poorly-aging classmates' wives we had been introduced to.

Apart from those who were in the Drama Club, we really didn't socialize with many of our schoolmates, and with the exception of the ones who used to come out on weekends to see our band, we really had nothing in common with anybody other than the fact we attended the same school. I was looking forward to seeing Mr. Mulroney and some of our old acting buddies. An "In Memoriam" table had been set up, giving honor to the startlingly high number of fellows who had left us. I didn't really care to delve into the sad details of each of their deaths, but it was heartbreaking, yet not surprising, to learn that both Robert Casey and Joseph Bonelli had died of aids. We knew forty-three years ago that they were "different."

Everybody present knew about us and our recent claim to fame. We must have been congratulated a thousand times and posed for at least a hundred pictures. We were, without question, the hit of the party. It was amazing how we suddenly had so many old friends who barely spoke to us then but now wanted to reconnect just because our faces happened to appear on their television screens. Much to our delight, Mr. Mulroney was among the faculty members who had attended the reunion. Forty years didn't leave much wear and tear on him; he looked almost as good as he did on the day we graduated. He was as thrilled to see us as we were to see him. We exchanged compliments and tried to squeeze forty years into thirty minutes. He told us he had retired from teaching, moved upstate to the town of New Paltz and opened a neighborhood bar with his brother-in-law.

"I've been seeing you guys regularly on TV," he said proudly, "You don't know how thrilled I was when I first recognized your three unforgettable faces!"

"Aw, thanks, Mr. M," Jack responded humbly, "We kind of owe it all to you. If it weren't for what you saw in us, who knows what we'd be doing!"

"From the first day I saw you three strutting down these very hallways," he declared, "I said to myself, 'These guys are destined to have their names in lights one day.'"

"That's nice of you to say," I answered graciously, "But if our names haven't been in lights by now, I doubt there's much of a chance of that ever happening!"

"Never say 'never'," he said with a prophetic smile, "Stranger things have happened!"

The reunion turned out to be a bittersweet affair. It was good to see some of the friendly faces of yesteryear, yet it was depressing to see so many of them looking so aged. As nice as it was to touch base with Mr. Mulroney, it was sad to think it could very well be the last time we'd ever see him. With our wives by our sides, the three of us exited the building, walking into the night like ghosts fleeing from the past and heading into the unknown.

John Rullo

~SEEING STARS~

    Starlight Agency was flooded with calls from curious media people wondering who the three exciting faces in the new Master Card commercial were. Executives at the credit card company were getting positive feedback about the ad, and signed on Sid and Phil to produce a series of commercials with the stipulation that we were in them. Pfizer pharmaceuticals had also put in a bid to use our faces in their newest Viagra advertisement. Finally feeling secure about his new career being financially rewarding, Willy decided to join Jack and me, submitting his papers to officially retire from the LIRR. Wendy had become a star in her own right, flaunting the fact she may have discovered the three biggest faces to ever hit Madison Avenue, but even she had no idea what was about to happen.
    Wendy had contacted each of us by phone, requesting a meeting with her as soon as possible. She had sent a limousine to pick us up at our homes in Long Island and deliver us to her office in Manhattan. She joyfully informed us how offers were pouring in from various advertisement agencies, modeling agencies, production companies and magazines faster than she could review them, and how important it was for us to make some decisions and help her in setting up what was soon to be our very busy schedule. Sitting in the back of a stretch limo with a stocked bar at our disposal, Willy poured three shots of Jack Daniels and toasted, "To us!" We clicked our shot glasses as Jack and I repeated in agreement, "To us!"

The Three Extras

For the first time since we had met Wendy, she seemed overwhelmed. She didn't want to turn down any offers, but she knew we were only human and could only be in one place at a time. It was imperative for her to know how we felt about traveling because quite a few of the projects she was lining up for us were being shot on location out of town…way out of town. One of the offers came from our old friends Sid and Phil. Based on the success of the Citifield commercial, Sid had come up with an idea for a campaign involving our three fresh faces traveling the country visiting all the major league baseball stadiums. Master Card loved the idea and everything was pending on whether or not we agreed to do it. Jack and Willy were much bigger sports fans than I was, so they wanted in the worst way to jump at the opportunity. As far as I was concerned, it would get me out of the house and present me with an opportunity to see the country. We signed on the dotted line and during the next year we flew to ten major US cities, visited ten major league ballparks, and established a reputation as the Stadium Guys. Our first shoot of the series took place at Boston's Fenway Park where one of the members of the make-up team suggested Jack wear a baseball cap because of his thinning hair. Phil loved the suggestion and from that day on, Jack was hardly ever seen without a cap on his head.

Our travel schedules were pretty hectic and every shoot went on for practically an entire day. After accompanying us on one of our stadium excursions, Tracy, Jenny, and Joanna decided they weren't having any fun as spectators and watching us get all the attention. Life on the road wasn't quite as glamorous as they had anticipated, so they never traveled with us on a business trip again. We were getting paid pretty well so it was no longer necessary for our wives to work, a little detail that made their resentment over our absence from home temporarily disappear.

Initially, they weren't very fond of the idea that each of us was able to retire while they couldn't. The new arrangements, however, were working out just fine; we got to travel while they got to spend our money. Besides, we all know what they say about absence making the heart grow fonder!

The Master Card commercials were getting a tremendous amount of air time. The television audience was anxiously awaiting what city and what ballpark the Stadium Guys were going to visit next. The campaign was really a stroke of marketing genius and all we were required to do was show up and pretend we were enjoying ourselves at a ball game. We never had to memorize a line or speak a single word. One restful afternoon in the spring of 2011, while we were all relaxing at home between shoots, more exciting news came our way from Wendy. She almost couldn't believe it herself. I answered my phone to the sound of her voice quivering with excitement, "Guess who I got a call from today!"

I was silent for a moment having no clue as to who she might have been referring to and then played along, "Uh, no clue, Wendy, give me a hint!"

"Just one of the biggest names in Hollywood, that's who! Martin Fuckin' Scorsese! Could you believe it? He wants the three of you to appear in his next film. No ifs ands or buts; he said no matter what it takes, it's you three he needs for a few scenes! Isn't that awesome?"

"How did he know about us?" I asked.

"He happened to see the Master Card ads and he absolutely loves you guys! I already spoke to Jack and Willy. I'm sending a car for you in the morning; you need to be in my office by ten! Do you have any idea what this could lead to?"

The Three Extras

Wendy was rambling away, her words flying off her tongue faster than I could process. "Okay, Wendy, slow down," I said laughing. "Great news, I'll see you tomorrow!"

The following morning, we were shaking hands with none other than Mr. Martin Scorsese. I was so tempted to go into my *Taxi Driver* bit, but Jack warned me ahead of time not to embarrass myself, or him for that matter. Scorsese was wearing his usual thick, black framed glasses and he was much shorter than I'd imagined. Standing practically a foot taller than the famous director made me feel awkward when having to look down to speak with him face to face.

"It's a real honor to meet you," I said as my eyes gleamed with admiration.

"Hey, I'm a regular Joe, no different than anybody else," he stated matter-of-factly, trying to put us at ease, "but I appreciate your respect." He appeared to be very fidgety, always in motion, pacing, tapping, and snapping his fingers. It was easy to imagine how his brilliant mind must have been entertaining a thousand thoughts a minute.

"Mr. Scorsese has something he wants to discuss with you," Wendy chimed in, taking on the role of self-appointed mediator, "The floor is yours, Mr. Scorsese!"

"Thank you, Wendy. You see fellows, you three have just the look I need for a few scenes in a new film I'm directing," he explained. "I'm telling you, it must be destiny. I rarely have the time to watch television, but as I was sitting in my barber's chair getting a trim, the second I saw your faces on his TV, I hollered, 'That's them!'" The celebrity's moves were inelegantly animated as he turned quickly, momentarily losing his balance while pointing his finger directly at our faces.

"We're flattered, Mr. Scorsese," Jack remarked, "Love your films. Just tell us when and where!"

"Call me Marty, screw the Mr. Scorsese shit!" he respectfully demanded as he circled the coffee table.

"Okay, Marty," Jack obliged, "We would be privileged to be a part of the new film!"

Marty perched himself on the arm of Wendy's couch and proceeded to fill us in with the details of his new project. He was about to begin production on a film entitled *Tenders*. It was a script especially close to his heart because it was written by his nephew, a character study about four distinctly unique individuals who dedicate their lives to tending bar. The movie was to be shot entirely on location in New York City and Los Angeles. All that was required of us was that we sit at a bar in each city and order drinks. Marty had already signed on James Franco, Jeff Bridges, Marisa Tomei, and Keanu Reeves to act in the lead roles, but he also had lined up a parade of stars to appear in cameos. It seemed as if no one in Hollywood ever said "No" to Martin Scorsese.

"My God!" Wendy squealed with schoolgirl delight, "Do you have any idea what an opportunity this is going to be for you boys? Do you realize how many celebrities you will meet in the making of this movie alone?"

"Relax, Wendy," Marty said, "They're just people! They put their pants on just the same as you and me."

"Sorry, Marty, I'm just excited for them," Wendy answered in a complete about-face of emotions. "I know you're a busy man," she continued in her business-like persona, "Have your office contact me with all the details and I'll see to it that The Three Extras report to work promptly, as needed."

Marty stood, we all shook hands, and we thanked him a million times over. He and Wendy shared a few last words as she walked him out to the elevator. The three of us stood there in the middle of Wendy's office not sure if what just occurred was a dream. "Pinch me," Willy yelped, "I can't fuckin' believe it; we're going to be in a Martin Scorsese movie!"

I started jumping up and down, thinking about how cool it was going to be to meet Marisa Tomei, making up nonsense rhymes like, "What a hap-hap-happy day, we're gonna meet Marisa Tomei!"

Jack, laughing out loud, said, "You're funny!"

"You said *I'm funny*. How the fuck am I *funny*, what the fuck is so *funny* about me?" I joked in my best Joe Pesci.

"You're such a fuckin' idiot," Willy lovingly criticized.

On that note, Wendy re-entered the room. "Is this fantastic or what?" she screamed, as her flip-flop of facial expressions returned to ecstatic joy. "In all my years in this business, I have never experienced anybody getting the attention you three unknowns are getting. It's absolutely astounding! Some kind of divine light is shining upon you three."

We returned home and took our wives out to yet another special dinner to deliver the great news. As excited as they appeared to be at first, in so many words, they made it known they weren't very thrilled about our newfound popularity or the news that we would traveling to Los Angeles again.

"I thought this being a movie extra was going to be just a part time thing," Jennifer complained, "This new career seems like it's taking up more of your lives than the jobs you left!"

"I'm sorry," Tracy added, "Your intentions were to be faceless extras on movie sets, not God damn celebrities!"

"Yeah," Joanna joined in, "What are we supposed to do while you guys are traveling around the country living it up? We're never gonna see you anymore!"

"You crack me up," I argued, "Living it up? We're working so you don't have to; you women are never happy!"

"Listen girls," Jack jumped in diplomatically, "This is not going to last forever. At most, we'll get another year out of it and if nothing else, we will have made some play money."

"Oh they're just worried that we're going to run off with some Hollywood starlets," Willy suggested.

"Oh yeah, right," Jenny blurted, "You old guys are every young actress's dream!"

"Are you talking to me?" I said, taking another shot at impersonating DeNiro.

"You're an idiot," Joanna groaned.

The dinner conversation ended up becoming a match of wits and an exchanging of digs instead of the congratulatory celebration we had expected. The truth of it was that the girls, although they refused to admit it, were jealous. We were suddenly no longer the homebodies readily available at their every beck and call. Although it was difficult for us to fathom how this fortuity seemed to happen overnight, there was no way we were going to give up the opportunity to travel, rub elbows with celebrities, and make some easy money. The girls were just going to have to grin and bear it.

Two weeks after the not so joyous dinner gathering, we received our instructions from Wendy and before we knew it were on a jet headed for LA. A limo waiting for us at LAX took us to the Grafton Hotel where Martin had left our itinerary for the week. We were given VIP treatment. Each of us had our very own luxury room with every accoutrement imaginable. Time after time I had to remind myself that I wasn't imagining all of this. Every morning at 8:30 we were to report to the set, a bar on West Sunset Boulevard called The Pomegranate. A full buffet

The Three Extras

breakfast was provided for the entire cast and crew, and the shooting began promptly at 10 AM. Marty was very regimented and stood firm about sticking close to schedule; he didn't tolerate tardiness. On the morning of our third day of shooting, Keanu Reeves showed up an hour late because he was hung-over and Scorsese threw a fit.

"There are a thousand other actors who want your part," he hollered, as he slammed his script down on the bar, "Don't come stumbling in here late again, you're not irreplaceable!"

"Marty, it won't happen again," Keanu said apologetically, acknowledging everyone in the room.

Our first day on the set, after the lighting crew had finished setting up the shots, the assistant director, a guy named Lucas, guided us to the far end of the bar where we were seated on three barstools. Lucas was the good little soldier, Martin's right arm, seeing to it that everything was running smoothly. Lucas had the unshaven Miami-Vice look. He sported brightly colored scoop-neck tee shirts that fit low enough to reveal a small patch of curly black chest hairs protruding from the top of the neck line. "Is this where you want them, Marty?" he called out, and the next thing we knew we were face to face with James Franco, who was standing behind the bar reading lines from the screenplay and getting into character. Lucas clearly explained to us that all we were expected to do was sit at the bar, nurse our drinks and nod affirmatively when Franco asked us if we were ready for another round. Every day for five consecutive days, we followed the same instructions and repeated what seemed to be the very same scenes. We nodded and sipped our drinks when cued, while witnessing the brilliance of Scorsese as he magically inspired his cast to create his vision.

Throughout the week, James Franco and Keanu Reeves alternated positions behind the bar. Franco gave the impression he was a very serious about his work. He followed Marty's orders to a tee and rarely interacted with anyone on the set except for those he was directly shooting a scene with. Keanu appeared to be more of a fun natured guy, easygoing and loose. On occasions, he would get silly, tell a joke, share an anecdote and treat us as if we were old friends. It was pretty exciting for us to see several of Hollywood's biggest names stop in to shoot cameo scenes. Among them were Scarlett Johansson, Cameron Diaz, Steve Buscemi and Dustin Hoffman. Most of the stars who agreed to appear in cameo roles gave the impression they were in a hurry and much too busy to hang around. At different times during the day, a limousine would pull up to the bar and drop off the actor or actress who would slip past the crowd of fans and make his or her grand entrance. The manner in which Marty showed his appreciation for the actors who agreed to do cameos was to accommodate them by quickly shooting their scenes so they could be on their merry way. Scarlett was absolutely gorgeous, very professional but a bit standoffish. She spoke only to Martin, didn't make eye contact with anyone except for the actors she was sharing a scene with. She inspired me to write a song about her, which I never completed; the words of the chorus went, "I wish I were young and handsome so I could date Scarlett Johansson." Cameron Diaz, on the other hand, chose to hang out at the bar for a while and during one of our breaks actually came over to sit with us. She was very bubbly, friendly and looked absolutely amazing.

"What's up guys?" she asked as she took a seat at our table, "I'm Cameron!"

"Hey, we certainly know who you are! I'm Jack and these are my partners in crime, Willy and Johnny."

"Nice to meet you guys," she said with the most engaging smile, "You three look so familiar; I know I've seen you before. It's got to come to me soon or it's gonna drive me crazy!" She took a sip of her beer and then burst out with a sigh of relief, "I know! You're the guys in those Master Card commercials!"

"That's us," Willy proudly acknowledged, happy to be recognized while trying not to appear star struck, "We're the Stadium Guys, professionally known as the Three Extras!"

"How very cool it is to meet you!"

"Likewise!" we simultaneously chimed in return.

Cameron chatted with us for almost thirty minutes, sharing some of her funny Hollywood stories, including one in which she admitted to almost killing Christian Slater on the set of *Very Bad Things* when her foot accidentally slipped off her car's brake pedal and hit the accelerator. "If it weren't for his being alert and able to jump out of the way, I would have crushed him," she confessed. We were right in the middle of telling her about some of the films we made in college when her cell phone rang. She politely excused herself, took the call and then told us she had to run. "Nice talking with you, Three Extras. Maybe we'll get to work together one day!" She rose from her seat and as she headed towards the exit, our eyes were affixed to the way her white Capri pants clung to her perfect body.

Willy let out with a long sigh, "My God," he whimpered, "How would you like to be tapping that ass?"

"Willy, I think she liked you," Jack teased, "Didn't you notice how she kept looking you over?"

"Yeah right," Willy laughed, as the twinkle in his eyes expressed how he wished Jack wasn't kidding.

"Did I ever tell you why I think she chose the name Cameron Diaz?" I asked my two friends.

"No, I don't think so, but I know you're about to," replied Jack.

"Camera-on-the-ass, get it? Cameron Diaz, pronounce it slowly…camera-on-the- ass!"

"She was friendly enough, why didn't you ask her?"

"Are you crazy, and spoil it for Willy?"

"Fuck you guys!"

After the fifth day of shooting, Marty said he had taken all the shots he needed, congratulated us for doing an outstanding job and reminded us he would see us again in New York City in two weeks. Even though we regarded Scorsese as a genius, at one point, we had no clue as to his methods of putting a film together because all the shots seemed to be so random and haphazard. But what did three guys from Queens know? Film-making technology had come a long way since the days we made movies in college. Computers certainly changed the look of editing room floors.

The night we were waiting for our plane to board at LAX was when we first experienced the thrill of getting recognized in public. Seated among our carry-on luggage and several other red-eye passengers, the three of us were discussing the events of the week when the two teenage children from a family sitting directly across from us started to point and whisper.

"Mom, Dad, I've seen those three guys on TV," mumbled the daughter.

"Don't stare!" the mother reprimanded.

"Should I go ask them?" the son asked.

"No! Don't embarrass us," murmured the dad, "They're probably nobodies!" not realizing we could clearly hear every word they were saying.

We just sat there grinning and allowed them to keep wondering, because at that point, we really were nobodies, just three guys in a few commercials. Nonetheless, it was quite the kick to be noticed.

    The return flight to JFK was smooth and uneventful. We had so much fun in Los Angeles all we could think about was getting back on the set in lower Manhattan. We were definitely going through the infatuation stage of show business, loving every minute of it. Our lives suddenly seemed to reclaim their purpose, our creative juices had been resurrected and a much needed confidence boost had us feeling the way we did when we were playing in Electric Dust. We felt energized and alive. When we were at home we felt life was stagnant and couldn't be bothered with the cares and the chores of everyday life. Jack, Willy and I were on the phone with each other constantly. Sometimes we had to convince ourselves that the entertainment business had really become part of our lives again. Sometimes our anxious curiosity had us asking each other repeatedly if there had been any news from Wendy. And sometimes we just needed to share with each other the gripes coming from our bored and discontented wives. When we were on the movie set, we were pampered. We were meeting interesting people and having stimulating conversation. Home life just wasn't as fulfilling. When Joanna tried to discuss domestic issues with me, although it was exceedingly unfair to her, I just wasn't interested. All I wanted to do was talk about who we met, who we were about to meet and how much I loved being involved in the movie business. The two week break in our schedule seemed eternal. I felt like a toddler waiting for Christmas Day to arrive. Wendy finally contacted us with our instructions for the New York shoot of *Tenders* and we were counting the minutes until we were back on the set.

"Shemp's" was a quaint New York City bar located downtown on Hudson off Spring Street. All throughout the premises were posters and photos of Shemp Howard, often referred to as "The Fourth Stooge." The proprietor was no relation to Shemp, nor did he have any connection to the family; the guy just had a strange fondness for him. We could have easily commuted back and forth from Long Island to Shemp's every day, but Mr. Scorsese insisted we be readily accessible and arranged to have us stay at the nearby Greenwich Hotel until shooting was complete, much to the displeasure of our wives who were quickly tiring of our very active lives away from home. Just like it had been in LA, we were getting treated royally in Manhattan. Meals, transportation or anything we so desired was graciously provided. For the life of us, we couldn't understand the attention and the celebrity treatment. It made no sense, we were merely no-name extras appearing in a few scenes and yet we were made to feel like movie stars. As crazy as it was, we played right along.

Marisa Tomei and Jeff Bridges had been cast in the roles of the New York bartenders. Everything was moving along rather smoothly, pretty much the same as it did on the west coast. Once again, Lucas was on hand to assist, directing us to our places at the bar and informing us that all we had to do was nod affirmatively when asked if we wanted another round. If ever there was a dream job, we had it. When we were working, life was almost like being on vacation. Enjoying the nightlife and staying in luxury hotels was something we easily got accustomed to.

Jeff Bridges was very private, keeping pretty much to himself. When he wasn't in front of the camera, he went his own way and did his own thing. He was very professional. He showed up on the set every morning exactly on time, knew his lines by heart, and was very courteous to everyone around him. He didn't say much more to us than good morning and good night, but was very pleasant in doing so. When Marty called it a wrap, Jeff mysteriously disappeared and nobody saw him until the next morning.

One evening as I was headed back to my hotel room, I had mistakenly gotten off the elevator at the wrong floor. Not realizing where I was, I walked along the corridor towards what I thought was my room, and heard the strumming of an acoustic guitar. I followed the sound to an open door and quietly stood outside to listen. When the playing stopped, I politely applauded at which point the door suddenly swung open to reveal none other than Jeff Bridges holding his guitar.

"Why thank you," he said grinning, "Just working on something; do you play?"

"Used to play quite a bit when I was younger; don't get the chance to pick it up too often."

Jeff extended his free hand and invited me in. "Excuse the mess," he mumbled while reaching for a guitar case that appeared as frayed and road weary as he did. He opened it carefully and slowly as if he were uncorking a bottle of vintage wine and resting inside was a 1960's classic Martin guitar in mint condition. He gently picked it up like it was a newborn, handed it over to me and said, "Check this baby out!" I sat on the edge of the left side of his unmade bed, softly strummed as he sat on the right side. The guitar played effortlessly and her tone was incredibly beautiful.

"G, F, and C; just follow me," he instructed in his signature gravelly voice. As soon as I caught on to the melody, I sang harmony with him on the choruses which led him to give me a big smile and a nod of approval. We ended the song together as if we'd been playing for years, "Pretty good man!

You know this one?" and he broke into Neil Young's "I Believe in You."

As the last note of the song rang out, he asked, "You indulge," after lighting up a joint and passing it over to me.

"Why not," I answered, "you go around once!"

I lost all sense of time as the two of us played through the night, taking turns suggesting songs and sucking down Bass Ales. We strummed, picked and faked the words we couldn't remember of one tune after another. He didn't say much, I didn't say much; the music did the talking.

"You sound great, man," he said enthusiastically to which I returned the compliment.

"Well, we don't want to piss off Mr. Scorsese, so I suppose we better get some shut eye," he wisely suggested. I reached out to shake his hand only to find his surprisingly tight grip pull me in close for a manly embrace and firm pat on the back. "It was a lot of fun my friend, a lot of fun!"

"I had a blast," I answered and stumbled my way out the door to hopefully find my room.

I had a remarkable time singing and playing that evening, not because of what we sounded like but because of who he was. I couldn't believe I was accompanying Jeff Bridges, the movie star, on guitar and vocals. There was no pretense with Jeff and even though we were just two guys jamming on an equal playing field, I remained a bit star struck. Nevertheless, the mystery of where he had been disappearing to every day was solved. I knew Willy and Jack were not going to believe me, so I never told them.

Marisa was a whole different story. She was not so mysterious and one of the friendliest, most outgoing women I'd ever met. She had spunk, a great sense of humor, and seemed like she was always up for a good time. She was also staying at the Greenwich and on a couple of nights she had asked if Jack, Willy and me cared to join her at the bar for a drink. How could we have refused? During those two nights, the four of us huddled around a quiet table in the corner and talked about everything from our meeting Jerry Garcia to George Costanza's fascination with her on Seinfeld. We explained all the circumstances leading to our involvement with Martin Scorsese and she apologized for not recognizing us.

"I'm sorry guys," Marisa confessed, "Whenever I watch television, which is extremely rare, I skip through the commercials, so there's no way I would have seen you."

"That's quite alright," Willy answered, smiling like a schoolboy with a crush, "TV is pretty much a waste of time; I hardly ever watch it myself!"

Willy was lying. He loved his DVR so he never had to miss his favorite shows, but to impress Marisa, he did what every man does; he lied! She made us feel as if we'd known her forever, and before we knew it, we were exchanging cell phone numbers. She seemed to really take to Willy, directing much of the conversation towards him, giving him high fives whenever she saw fit. During one of those up in the air hand slaps, she clasped her fingers around his and held on for a long enough time to make me suspect something was up. For one thing, Willy surprisingly wasn't wearing his ever present wedding ring, and for another, there were no signs of attachment on Marisa's fingers. One night as the four us were chatting away at what we claimed was "our table," I didn't realize how late it was getting until Jack said, "Never gonna get to the set on time tomorrow if I don't get some sleep!"

"Good idea," I agreed, "It's time to hit the hay; enough fun for one day!"

"You guys go on up," Willy instructed, "I'm gonna have one more drink; I'll be up soon!"

"That's the spirit," Marisa called out with a giggle, and gave Willy yet another high five followed by a kiss on the cheek which suddenly changed his skin tone to the color of her third strawberry daiquiri.

The following morning while the three of us were headed over to Shemp's, I interrogated Willy. "So what in the world was going on between you and Ms. Tomei last night, Mr. I Don't Watch Television?"

"Nothing," Willy squeaked, never making eye contact, "We just had another drink and a few more laughs."

"Bullshit, I saw the way she held on to your hand…she was flirting with you big time!"

"Get out of here," Willy barked, "What the fuck would Marisa Tomei want with Willy Taylor?"

"Why not," asked Jack, adding fuel to the fire, "You're a good looking, personable guy. I could easily see her being attracted to you especially since you weren't wearing a wedding ring!!"

"Would you guys please stop it," Willy pleaded, "We finished our drinks then called it a night and I took my ring off because my finger is swollen, it's too tight and extremely uncomfortable!"

"You slept with her, didn't you," I pressed.

"No, I did not and even if I did, I wouldn't tell you," he hissed unconvincingly, "And not a word of this gets to Tracy, you hear me!"

"So, you did sleep with her," I blurted out with a touch of envy, "Don't worry pal, your secret is safe with us, right Jack?!"

"My lips are sealed," Jack replied.

The Three Extras

"Fuck you, I didn't *sleep* with her!"

When we arrived on the set, Marisa was already there, looking as bright and lively as could be.

"Hey Willy," she called out cheerfully energetic, "You sleep well?"

Jack and I turned to each other and in what was an instant of astonishment and jealousy combined, he whispered, "He did sleep with her! Son of a bitch!"

Our week in New York City went rather well. We shot scenes with Jeff and Marisa and had very brief hello/goodbye encounters with Robert DeNiro, Tom Waits, Sarah Jessica Parker, and Tracy Morgan, as they quickly dropped by to shoot their cameos, their way of paying homage to Marty. All week long, Hudson Street was crawling with fans and curious onlookers hoping to catch a glimpse of a celebrity or possibly get an autograph. One sunny, gorgeous afternoon, Marisa had joined the three of us when we stepped outside of Shemp's to get a breath of fresh air. Almost immediately, we were approached by a group of six young star gazers who had instantly recognized Marisa.

"We love you, Marisa," they cried, while holding out sheets of paper and pens, pleading for autographs.

Two members of the group approached Jack, Willy and I and looked us over carefully. "Are you somebody?" one of them asked curiously.

"I think I'm somebody," Jack answered while adjusting his baseball cap, "Am I somebody, Marisa?"

As Marisa scribbled her name onto a sheet of yellow legal paper, she messed with the fans. "You mean you don't know who these three handsome fellows are?" she teased.

"They kind of look familiar," one of the girls replied.

"Why this is Willy Taylor, Jack Reilly and John Colletti," she announced proudly, and as if she had a peek into the future, she continued, "These three gentlemen are on their way to becoming major stars. Get their autographs now so you could say, 'I met them when!'"

Before we knew it, people were gathering all around as paper and pens were thrust at us from every direction. Marisa stood by, laughing as we signed autographs for over-enthusiastic movie fans who thought we might eventually become "somebody's" someday, based solely upon her unintentionally prophetic statement.

The week certainly seemed to fly by. When our scenes were completed and our presence no longer needed, Marty thanked us for our participation, cooperation, and hard work. He said it had been a delight working with us, told us we were free to go and we should expect a call from his office before long. As I stepped out of Shemp's for the last time, I heard a familiar voice cry out, "Good meeting you!" I quickly turned my head to see it was Jeff Bridges from the back window of a taxi giving me a wink and a thumbs-up as it pulled away from the curb.

"Likewise," I hollered, raising my two fingers with the peace sign.

"What was that all about?" Jack and Willy wondered out loud.

"If I told you guys that Jeff and I spent an evening in his room singing, playing guitar and smoking pot, would you believe me?"

"I still don't believe any of this," Willy said. "You could tell me anything!"

"Guess he must have liked working with us, what else could it be?" Jack remarked as if he didn't hear what I said.

The Three Extras

"He doesn't really say too much, does he?" I asked as we strolled north on Hudson in the midst of countless pedestrians who had no clue we were headed for fame and fortune.

Marisa was standing at the desk in the hotel lobby as a bellboy was helping us load our luggage into the trunk of our limo. Dressed in jeans, sandals and a well-worn Neil Young sweatshirt, she came busting through the hotel's front door like in a scene from a movie, "Hey," she cried out, "Aren't you guys going to say goodbye?" She gave each of us a hug and a kiss on the cheek and told us what a pleasure it had been meeting and working with us. She then directed her attention entirely on Willy, looked him over, smiled and said, "Call me sometime!"

One by one, to avoid bumping our heads, the three of us ducked as we climbed into the back of the limousine. Willy was the last one to enter as Marisa pushed the door shut behind him. As the car pulled away from the curb, Willy waved and Marisa blew a kiss. For at least two city blocks, Jack and I silently stared at Willy as he seemed to be lost in thought, completely oblivious to anything and anyone around him.

"What?" he hollered as his head turned to catch us ogling, "What are you looking at?"

"You!" we shot back.

"You're like a lovesick little schoolboy," I said.

"She's so nice," Willy sighed like a student with a crush on his teacher.

"Lots of people are nice," Jack snapped, "I'm nice, Johnny's nice, Tracy's nice. What we want to know is did you sleep with her?"

"Gentlemen never tell; I'll take it with me to the grave," Willy answered with a secretive grin. Jack, me, and Ramon, the eavesdropping limo driver, laughed and silently drew our own conclusions.

The Three Extras

John Rullo

~IT COMES WITH THE TERRITORY~

    Getting a little taste of Hollywood and the movie star lifestyle certainly made living in the suburbs of Long Island seem dull, boring and monotonous. Unless it was about my kids, I could not have cared less about anything except news of our next job. I loved traveling, I loved being pampered and I especially loved getting paid for it. At the outset, Joanna was on board and thrilled about the new chapter in the lives of me and my two best friends, but little by little she began to show signs of resentment. She hated not having me at home to share in all the domestic issues, but at that stage of our lives, I just didn't care anymore. I was totally preoccupied with show biz. Jack was going through a similar situation with Jennifer. He was so caught up in the excitement of our new careers he completely ignored Jenny and her needs. Willy, on the other hand, was showering Tracy with attention and affection, which Jack and I were certain had to be his way of alleviating the guilt of his obsession with Marisa Tomei.
    Within two weeks of the shooting of *Tenders*, Willy received an unexpected yet promising phone call from Marisa. Darren Aronofsky, director of the movie *The Wrestler*, just so happened to be discussing with her the subject of his next film project and mentioned how he was seeking new and interesting faces for what would be non-speaking roles. We immediately came to Marisa's mind so she strongly suggested he consider The Three Extras. On Marisa's suggestion, he decided it would

probably be worth his while to meet with us and as a favor, he requested she set it up.

It was hard to believe a little over two years had passed since the day we met Wendy Levine. Time was a blur as long as we were keeping busy. It was even harder to believe how three retired suburbanites from Long Island could be sitting at a Starbucks in Manhattan with Marisa Tomei and Darren Aronofsky making arrangements to appear in yet another major motion picture. Darren was comfortably dressed in jeans and a blue denim button down shirt with the sleeves rolled up to his elbows. He was much taller than I had expected. He stood about six feet tall, had a great physique, and appeared to be extremely health conscious. He was sipping on a large Chai tea while casually studying our faces. He struck me as the type of person who was convinced about what he wanted; determined, confident and quick-witted.

"So you fellows worked with Martin Scorsese," he asked, "Great guy, isn't he?"

"It was a pleasure watching him in action," Jack replied, trying to carry himself as professionally as possible, "A wonderful person, I can see why he is so well liked!"

Darren quickly checked a text message on his phone, and then returning his attention to us, commented, "Yeah, Marty's brilliant, I want to be just like him when I grow up!" We all shared in the laugh and then as if by a flip of a switch, his attitude turned serious as he proceeded to give us a detailed synopsis of the movie. The working title of his film was *Sedona* and it was based on a couple of deranged old hippies who settle in Arizona and recruit susceptible members of their generation by duping them into joining a rather bizarre New Age cult. We were to be cast as three naïve followers who get conned into enlisting in the program. Darren explained how he was more concerned about our look than our acting ability and reassured us his assistants would be on hand to coach us along.

"In most of your scenes I will need you boys to appear as though you are in a trance," he informed us, "a little bit more entailed than being just an extra, but from what Marisa tells me, you three are naturals!"

"We can do that," Jack reassured him as everyone laughed, "Kind of feel like that a lot lately, anyway."

The movie was to start production a few weeks later on location in Sedona, Arizona. Darren expressed his approval repeatedly by stating we had the perfect faces for the parts and mentioned several times how pleased he was to be working with us. Marisa was delighted that she could be the liaison between Darren and us, and in a repeat performance, couldn't let go of Willy's hand as she cried out, "I'm so happy for you guys!" Life just kept getting better. It was the year of our sixtieth birthdays and we were feeling as if we were back in our twenties.

Airports had begun to feel like home for us. Once again, we were boarding a jet, this time to Flagstaff, Arizona. When we arrived in Flagstaff, we were picked up by a stretch limousine and taken directly to The Enchantment Hotel in Sedona, a far cry from a Holiday Inn or Best Western. Our rooms had every amenity we could imagine, from a Jacuzzi tub to an espresso machine, along with breathtaking balcony views of the rust-red mountains enhanced by the intense colors of millions of flowers, juniper trees and cactus. It was too bad Joanna, Tracy and Jenny didn't join us on this trip; they would have had a splendid time without ever leaving the hotel.

We arrived in Sedona on a Sunday afternoon and shooting wasn't scheduled to begin until Wednesday morning. Darren had told us how he liked his cast and crew members to acclimate to the surroundings and settle in before getting to work. That evening, Willy, Jack and I decided to have a few drinks at the hotel bar. Entering the bar was like crossing the threshold into another world. The décor and the ambiance were conducive to unwinding and forgetting about the world outside, almost floating us into another dimension. Dreamlike lighting created a tranquil mood, while crystals dangled from the arcing oaken beams which held the glass panel ceiling in place. The staff was extremely friendly and extremely accommodating.

"Are you fellows involved with the film crew?" a charming young waitress inquired.

"Uh, yes we are!" I replied, "We are actors with very small parts; but you know what they say, 'There are no small parts, just small actors,' or is it the other way around? 'There are no small actors, just small parts?'"

"Don't mind him," Jack interjected, "We're movie extras hired by Mr. Aronofsky and good friends of Marisa Tomei. Maybe you've seen us in the Master Card commercials?"

"I knew you three looked familiar! That's right! You're the guys who go to all the baseball stadiums! Now I'm relieved; it would have driven me crazy wondering where I've seen you before! Let me get you guys a table."

She sat us at a table by a window with a striking view of the red rocks, blue waterfalls and vibrant foliage.

"Oh my God," Willy cried out, "This is freakin' amazing!"

"It's good to be us," I said, raising my hand for a return high five from my partners.

Right at the same time the waitress was taking our drink order, I noticed Julianne Moore had stepped foot into the room.

"Look guys," I said raising my voice and pointing like a star-struck tourist, "Look who just walked into the bar."

"Don't point, you idiot," Jack reprimanded, "You're going to embarrass us!"

"Miss Moore is a guest at the hotel," the waitress disclosed, "I believe she's here filming a movie also. I'll be right back with your drinks!"

Since Darren never told us who would be starring in *Sedona*, we put two and two together and guessed Julianne Moore was one of his stars. Next thing we knew, our waitress was talking with the actress and pointing towards us. I've always loved Julianne and the roles she played, and when I saw her heading directly for our table, I couldn't contain my excitement. "Holy shit," I muttered, "Julianne-fucking-Moore!"

"Hey guys, mind if I join you," she asked with a warm, charming smile.

"Not at all," I answered ecstatically, clumsily and hastily grabbing a chair and motioning for her to take a seat, "Make yourself comfortable!"

We spread our chairs around the table in a combined effort to give the actress some room as our waitress strode over with a bottle of red wine. She poured Julianne a small amount just enough to taste. We watched as she slowly swirled the wine about in her glass, admiring its legs and passionately breathing in the bouquet. She sipped the wine, closed her eyes and smiled with approval, "Ooh wow, this is really good." Julianne thanked our waitress who left the bottle at the center of the table, and then after taking another sip, she directed her conversation at us, "So, I hear you fellows are here to take part in Darren's film?"

"Yes we are," Jack humbly informed her, "but only in small roles in a few scenes; we're kind of in the background…"

"Don't belittle yourselves," she said encouragingly, "Darren is an artist, very selective about who appears in every

The Three Extras

scene of his films. You're here because you have the certain something he has in mind."

"That's very kind of you to say," I told her, "I assume you're playing a major part."

"It's got nothing to do with being kind, it's just the way it is," she stated, "and yes, I'm playing the role of Madeline, one of the women in Kevin Spacey's life."

"You mean Kevin Spacey is in the movie too?" Willy asked, excitedly anticipating the response.

"Why yeah," she answered surprised, "Darren never told you who was starring in the film?"

"No, he just told us to show up here and we would find out all the particulars when the time came. What else can you tell us?"

"Maybe I said too much already," she chuckled, "Don't want Darren getting pissed off at me! Hey, you guys should try this wine. It's extraordinary."

By elegantly raising her hand, Julianne signaled for our waitress and instantly she appeared. "Could you bring three more wine glasses and while you're at it, another bottle. This stuff is killer!"

To me, Julianne Moore was absolutely gorgeous. Her eyes shone with a positive glimmer and her smile was as beautiful as it was uplifting. She was comfortably dressed in loose fitting jeans, sandals and a Lucinda Williams 2006 tour date tee shirt. I've always admired Julianne and could not believe I was sitting at the table with her sharing a bottle of incredible wine and discussing one of my favorite singer/songwriters.

"So, you're a Lucinda fan?" I asked.

"Big time!" she answered with a sparkle in her eyes, "and you?"

"Have all of her CD's and seen her in concert half dozen times!"

"'Car Wheels on a Gravel Road' is still her best," she insisted without an argument from me.

The four of us were having the nicest time, discussing Julianne's films and telling her all about the history of our friendship, including the tales of our band, our college films, our jobs, and our newfound career as movie extras. We were already on our third bottle of wine and feeling pretty good when Julianne's attention was suddenly caught by to two ladies who had just entered the bar. "Oh, you're going to love these girls," she said as she sprung up from her seat gesturing for them to come over. "Jack, Willy, Johnny…meet Lori and Fran!"

We stood up to greet the newcomers, pulled over a couple more chairs and our growing party continued. Julianne convinced her friends to sample the wine and our attentive waitress was right over with two more glasses and another two bottles. Lori and Fran were both extremely beautiful women, who obviously took very good care of themselves. Fran, the taller of the two, maybe five/eight, had a healthy Arizona tan, long blond hair tied back in a braid, sunglasses resting above her brow and the deepest green eyes. She was wearing sandals, snug faded jeans and a loose fitting sky-blue cotton shirt opened to the waist with a black tank top underneath.

Lori stood about five/five. Her silky black hair was shaped with precision, cut just above her shoulders with long bangs that bordered her dark brown eyes. The southwest sun deepened her olive complexion, exaggerated even more so by her yellow sundress. She had a soft voice, an infectious giggle and immediately gave me the impression she knew how to appreciate life.

The Three Extras

"Lori, Fran and I have been friends since we were teenagers," Julianne explained, "They live here in Arizona and since I was going to be in town, there was no way we weren't going to hook up!"

After a few more glasses of wine, everyone had loosened up considerably, joking, laughing and revealing bits and pieces of their life stories. Lori, who hailed from Flagstaff, was co-owner of a wellness center there. She had a string of serious relationships but never married and currently was unattached. Fran, who lived in nearby Winslow, was divorced. She was once married to a very successful land developer with whom she had one child, a son. They parted on good terms and he left her with enough money to live extremely well for the rest of her life.

Jack, Willy and I were undeniably caught up in the moment. We were two thousand miles away from home, in the company of attractive, intriguing women, and somehow, after another bottle of wine, the images of our trusting wives standing guard in our consciences were steadily vanishing. Since the day Joanna and I started dating, I had never been unfaithful, but that night, all my inhibitions had been lifted and with the right combination of alcohol and coaxing, I was aware anything could happen.

We were having such a strangely fantastic time joking, listening to and telling stories, that before long we felt as if we've known Julianne and her friends forever. Up above, through the glass ceiling, the Arizona night sky was breathtaking. I couldn't recall ever seeing so many dazzling stars. Lori suggested we get some fresh air by taking a walk outside to check out the hotel's amazing landscaping. Willy and I were game for anything and thought it sounded like a great idea. Jack, in spite of the festive spirit filling the room, was feeling tired. As much as he would try to keep up with us, after a certain hour, his energy would fade. He made it a point not to push himself too hard and he'd already had more to drink in one night than he's had in years. "You guys go ahead," he said, "I think I'm gonna settle in." Just then, Julianne got a call on her cell and without explaining why, she insisted we go on ahead without her and she would catch up later. With Jack calling it a day and Julianne tending to personal business, Willy and I were left alone with Fran and Lori for a walk in the starlight. It wasn't until I first stood up that I realized how pleasantly buzzed I'd become. My first few steps were a little wobbly and Lori must have found it a perfect excuse to lock arms with me. Willy and Fran followed closely behind and I could only imagine what must have been going on in Willy's head. We slowly walked the grounds of the hotel, admiring the vivid colors of the blooming flowers and lively plants. The moon was bright and full, obediently hanging in the blackness of space just below a blanket of flickering stars.

"Isn't the sky incredible?" Lori asked, humbled by its magnificence, "I could never get tired of this!"

At that point I would have agreed to anything, even though I could not deny the view was extremely amazing and humbling. "Fuckin' awesome," I mumbled, my words slightly slurred, betraying that I had too much to drink. We walked beside a three feet high brick wall that surrounded a flourishing garden of assorted herbs.

"Let's sit for a few minutes," Lori suggested, and we followed her lead, taking seats on the wall beside her. The fragrance filling the air from the various aromatic plants was intoxicating. She reached into her compact leather pocketbook and pulled out a small pipe which I recall was used for smoking hash back in the day.

The Three Extras

"Anybody up for a hit?" she asked while unveiling a small rust colored chunk from inside a piece of tin foil.

"I haven't seen that stuff in over thirty years," I marveled with a mild slur, "I didn't think you could get that shit anymore!"

"You can get anything you want at Alice's Restaurant," she quipped.

Willy's eyes lit up. "Oh man," he cautioned, "Are we going to be able to walk after smoking this shit?"

"Oh, this stuff is nice and mellow," Lori assured us as she flicked on her lighter to ignite the magic morsel. She inhaled slowly as the piece of hash glowed fiery orange and then passed the pipe along to me. There was no one else in sight as the four of us sat side by side like reckless thrill-seeking teenagers below a captivating Arizona nightscape, surrounded by a multitude of glimmering heavenly lights, getting ridiculously stoned.

I had no idea where Willy and Fran eventually disappeared to that night or how Lori and I managed to find our way to my hotel room. I hadn't been that stoned since I was in my twenties. For a moment in time, John Colletti, retired blue collar worker from Suburbia, Long Island, was on a magic carpet ride. It was wonderfully surreal to feel cushioned by air as I fell back onto my bed, gliding gracefully downward until being engulfed by its sinking softness. Lori slipped out of her yellow sundress and seemed to dreamily drift down until her soft body was entwined with mine. She began kissing me on the lips and as wonderful and exciting as it felt, signals from my fast fading conscience were causing me to resist.

"What's the matter," Lori moaned, "Doesn't it feel nice?"

As if one fine thread was trying to drag me back into reality, I murmured, "You know, I'm married."

Lori giggled, and as she nibbled on my neck, whispered, "Hey baby, why should anyone deprive themselves of what feels so good?" She kissed my ear and softly sang, "If you can't be with the one you love, honey, love the one you're with!" At that point, anything she said would have made sense to me. The thread snapped and I simply surrendered to her irresistible advances. From playfully tumbling about in bed to soaking together in the bubbling warm water of the Jacuzzi, everything was strangely intensified. Whatever we smoked heightened every sense except for my sense of guilt. As the rising sun broke through my window the following morning, exhausted from submitting to a night of unrestrained intense pleasure, we fell sound asleep in each other's arms.

It was noon on Monday when the blaring of the hotel room phone startled me, waking me from a deep sleep. In a drowsy stupor I reached over and clumsily felt about for the receiver. "Hello," I grumbled, looking over to see Lori's lovely body sleeping naked beside me.

"Are you okay?" Jack's concerned voice vibrated in my head, "Joanna's been calling your cell phone all morning…"

"Oh shit!" I whispered, already trying to calculate how to wriggle my way out of my predicament, "I don't even know where I put my cell phone!"

"She called Jenny when she couldn't reach you," Jack explained, "and Jenny, in turn, called me hoping to get to you. I told her your phone died and you were in the shower…Where the fuck were you anyway? You didn't…"

"I'll fill you in later," I snapped in a slight panic and hung up the phone.

As the noonday sunlight beamed upon Lori's body, she stretched and her eyes slowly opened to catch me staring at her loveliness, causing my sudden moment of panic to miraculously subside. Smiling, she reached out her arms and motioned for me to lie beside her, our bodies once again fitting together like matching puzzle pieces. "One for the road?" she asked, as she rolled over and placed herself tenderly on top of me. Although maintaining a pleasant high undoubtedly heightened our dreamlike encounter, it had been years since I experienced the kind of powerful passion Lori and I shared all throughout the previous evening. I felt like I could have easily become abnormally addicted to her, yet I knew she was a free spirit, one of those seize the moment kind of people. Just as quickly and mysteriously as she entered my life, she'd be gone, leaving me with just a fond memory. She was a no strings attached kind of woman, with a contagious life-loving spirit, who captured my heart and imagination and whose intentions were only to move on.

While Lori showered, I scoured the room for my cell. I found it under the pile of our clothes and then dialed Joanna. Shamefaced, I felt absolutely horrible having to contrive a believable story to explain my whereabouts and why I didn't answer my phone. As much as I didn't regret a second of the time I spent with Lori, I hated myself for lying to my wife. Joanna and I used to turn a hotel room inside out, but somehow as we grew older, just like most old married couples, we lost the spark and started to take each other for granted. We forgot who we were and what it was that attracted us to each other. Lori was all about having a good time and she brought back those feelings, making me feel sexually alive again. Wrapped in a towel, she walked from the bathroom towards the bed. I had just gotten off the phone with Joanna and I guess she could tell from the look on my face I was a bit dismayed.

"What's the matter, sweetheart?" she asked as she ran her fingers through her wet hair.

"Oh, you know, I guess the love the one you're with approach is wreaking a little havoc on my conscience."

"You regret what we did?"

"Not for a minute," I said, as she took a seat beside me on the bed and held onto my hand.

"You go around once, my friend. We shared a beautiful time together. If ever we should meet up again, maybe the same magic will strike. I don't expect anything more from you, nor should you expect anything more from me. Nobody has to know but the two of us!"

She leaned over, picked her clothes out from the pile on the floor, and, while slipping into her dress, she said, "What do you say we go grab a bite to eat. I don't know about you, but I'm starving!"

After I showered and dressed, I called Willy. He and Jack were sitting at the pool wondering if and when I was ever going to come out from my room.

"You guys hungry?" I asked, "You want to meet Lori and me in the restaurant for some breakfast…uh, lunch, or whatever…"

"We had breakfast about four hours ago; it's almost dinner time, for God's sake!" Willy noted sarcastically. "And by the way," he went on, "We just saw Julianne and Fran; they asked if either of us had seen Lori because she hasn't been answering her phone either; we assumed she had to be with you?"

"Lunch, breakfast, dinner, brunch, whatever," I barked, "Do you want to eat or not? And yes, Lori's with me and what happens in Sedona stays in Sedona!"

Lori made contact with Fran and Julianne, and along with Jack and Willy, we all met for lunch on the outdoor patio of the hotel's amazing restaurant. It was a beautiful afternoon; the

The Three Extras

sun was in full bloom, the smell of citrus filled the air and there wasn't a cloud to be seen in the powder blue Arizona sky.

"So, I hope everyone had as much fun last night as we did," Lori said smiling wryly as her eyes eagerly scanned the menu, "Ooh, this looks good!"

"What did I miss?" Julianne inquired with a smirk, as if she knew her friend better than to ask.

"If I recall correctly," I remarked, "I think we all got a little too wasted."

"Sorry I missed all the fun," Jack said, and then directed his next comment to me, "but I went to my room, called my wife, and watched a movie." Shifting his attention to Julianne, he continued, "I finally got to see The Kids Are Alright. You were outstanding!"

"Thank you Jack," Julianne replied graciously, "I had a wonderful time making that picture."

Thanks to Jack's compliment, the conversation segued into critiquing Julianne's movie and opened up a discussion on gay marriage.

"I loved it too," Lori spoke from behind her menu, "Julianne was fabulous. Did you ever get to see that old movie about the gay cowboys?"

"It's crazy how I just couldn't get into Brokeback Mountain," Jack quickly responded. "It wasn't so much the part about two men having sex that bothered me; it was the cheating on the spouse part. The Kids Are Alright, however, I found to be totally gratifying!"

"That's because, like you, most men fantasize about beautiful lesbians," Willy commented, "remember the film we made in college?"

"You made a lesbian movie in college," Fran asked, "Way ahead of your time, don't you think?"

"Yeah, that's us, always ahead of our time, never on time," I joked, hoping the topic of conversation would stray as far away as possible from the events of the previous evening.

Then, thank goodness, right in the middle of our in-depth exchange of opinions, none other than Kevin Spacey strolled over to our table. His portrayal of Lester Burnham in *American Beauty* made him one of my favorite actors. He was wearing a raggedy old pair of jeans, sandals and a much worn out pre-Joe Walsh Eagles tee-shirt.

"Julianne!" he called out from a few feet away, "The script is amazing! I think we have a hit in the making!" Julianne stood and greeted Kevin with a passing hug and kiss on the cheek.

"Kevin," she said, directing his focus to all of us sitting around the food-filled table, "Let me introduce you to some friends of mine! This is Fran and Lori, two dear and longtime friends who just so happen to live here in Arizona; and these three gentlemen are Jack, Willy and John, who will be appearing as extras in a few scenes with us!"

"So nice to meet you," he said while examining our faces closely. "You three guys look so familiar, I know I've seen you somewhere!"

Julianne solved the mystery for him. "The three baseball fans in the credit card commercials!"

"Damn! You're right," he yelped, "Do you guys have any idea how captivating your faces are? Those commercials are awesome! There's just something magically magnetic about you three; no wonder why Darren wants you in his film!"

"You're so right Kevin. Uh, is it okay if I call you Kevin, Mr. Spacey?" Lori asked with a look that said "I'm going to call you Kevin anyway!" Then, while caressing my calf with her foot, immediately agreed, "I was drawn to them from the moment I saw them too!"

"You can call me anything you feel comfortable with my dear," Kevin courteously responded to Lori, "But as for you guys, take my word for it; your faces are, as they say, priceless! I'm sure we'll be seeing a lot of you three!"

Kevin excused himself, explaining how he had to meet some friends at the bar. Before walking away, he gave the ladies a friendly nod and told us how much he was looking forward to meeting again at Wednesday's shooting.

"Well I guess you three ladies have some catching up to do," Jack assumed.

"Yeah," Fran replied, "It was an absolute pleasure meeting you guys, but we haven't seen Julianne in years and we're out of here tonight."

As the busboys cleared the table, we rose from our chairs and bid our farewells to Lori and Fran. Lori handed me her business card, kissed me firmly on the mouth and said, "If ever you're in Flagstaff, give me a call!" Jack and Willy looked at each other and shook their heads in wordless wonder as Lori pulled me close in long tight embrace.

Julianne laughed and reminded her friend the clock was ticking. "So, Lori, who did you come here to spend time with?"

As Julianne and her two friends walked off into the distance, Willy and Jack simultaneously demanded, "What the fuck went on between you two last night?"

I pleaded my case. "Guys, she got me so wasted, shit, I felt like I was seventeen again! I had no idea how we even ended up back in my room, never mind how we wound up sleeping together. Whatever we were smoking…"

"For Christ's sake, John, at one point you had to realize that you're married to Joanna," Willy interrupted.

"Believe me, at one point I had no idea who I was or where I was; besides, what the hell are you talking about? I'm pretty sure you must've spent the night with Fran!" I said in a frantic weak defense for my actions.

"You guys wandered off with the pipe! We just walked around the grounds for a while assuming you went back to the bar. We had another drink and then called it a night. As much as I would have liked to have banged Fran…"

"Hey man, wait a second! How can you point a finger at me after you were messing around with Marisa Tomei? You think we didn't know what was going on with you guys, acting like two horny high school kids?"

"Come on! I think she's hot and all, and we may have flirted a lot, but I didn't fuckin' sleep with her!"

"All right, guys, let's drop it!" Jack firmly advised, "Nothing happened and nobody brings it up again! Understood?"

The three of us shook hands and Willy and I repeated, "Understood!"

On a picture perfect Wednesday morning, we boarded the luxury bus that was waiting outside our hotel, and it took us, along with members of the cast and crew, to the location of the shoot. When we arrived at the set, not even a twenty minute drive from the hotel, Darren Aronofsky was already there, and lighting and camera crews were setting up the necessary equipment to shoot the day's scenes. Kevin and Julianne were sitting beside each other sipping coffee and reviewing the script. We were patiently awaiting our instructions, because the truth was, we were relatively clueless as to what we were expected to do. As we were watching, paying close attention to all the behind the scenes activity, a young, energetic woman by the name of Mattie came from out of the blue and introduced herself as Darren's assistant. Simply put, she was stunningly beautiful, and in a take charge manner asked if we would kindly follow her to a nearby trailer. We would have followed her anywhere regardless of Jack's constant reminders that she was young enough to be one of our daughters. It was there that she left us in the hands of the make-up and wardrobe crew. After our faces had been degreased and made camera-ready, we were given white robes, the attire needed to be worn by us in our first scene. Throughout the day, Mattie and Darren painstakingly guided us along. We were told where to stand, where to sit, how to walk, and what emotions to express. We were basically moved about like stage props while Kevin and Julianne acted out their parts in what I thought were Academy Award performances. It was interesting to note how Darren's method of directing was very different from that of Martin Scorsese, yet each drew amazing results from their actors. Jack, Willy and I went about the long day ready at all times to take our places on the set eager to follow whatever orders the director had for us, with assistance from Maddie. Most of our scenes were accomplished in one take and Darren, Julianne and Kevin made it known, more than once, what a joy it was to work with us. They described us as "professional, courteous, cooperative, extremely photogenic, charming and captivating." We ate it up.

Throughout the week, it felt as if scenes were being shot so unsystematically, bouncing from one location to the next, it became terribly difficult making heads or tails of the process or the story. By no means were we well-versed with all the angles of filmmaking, so we simply trusted it would all come together in the editing room. We had been on hand and camera-ready for a total of ten days when Darren and Mattie informed us that all of our scenes had been shot and we were at last free to go. They wished us well and expressed their joy at working with us and hoped to repeat the experience again soon. It was a bit depressing to know our work was done, and we departed feeling somewhat like players who just got eliminated from a reality show. We had developed a special bond with Julianne. Somehow she made us feel as if we've been lifelong friends. Kevin joined her in bidding us adieu and made sure to mention how he hoped we were planning to attend the movie's premier.

Being part of the making of *Sedona* was an extremely rewarding experience. We learned a great deal about moviemaking and met numerous friendly, interesting people, but as I've often heard it spoken, we seemed to be in the world, not of it. Those ten days of non-stop action were long and demanding. The schedule was tight, allowing very little time for the informality and the socializing we encountered when we had first arrived. As the three of us sat in seats A, B, and C of row 9, flight 1210 to New York, we sat quietly, contemplating the events of the past two weeks, wondering how we were ever going to adjust to life back home.

New York welcomed us with grey and gloomy skies. At any minute it looked as though the heavens were going to open up and pelt us with rain. Our limo crawled in bumper to bumper traffic along the Belt Parkway on route to our homes and already I was missing Sedona. I was experiencing some guilt-ridden anxiety about facing Joanna and asked Willy if he would accompany me into my home as a buffer. For some reason, I thought she was going to see right through me and know.

"How's she going to know," Willy asked, "You're being needlessly paranoid!"

"Women just seem to know! They can sense things, especially when infidelity's involved!"

"You're worried over nothing. Next time you should think before you mess around with another woman!" Willy scolded.

Jack's house was our first stop. Jenny stood waiting on the front porch as Willy and I helped him unload his luggage. The sky grew even darker as the three of us walked briskly along the red brick path leading to his door. Jack patted me on the shoulder, laughed a sympathetic laugh and said, "Don't worry, Johnny boy! What happened in Sedona will stay there!" Jack and Jenny waved from the window as Willy and I darted back towards the car, trying to avoid the raindrops the sinister clouds had just begun to unleash.

By the time we arrived at my house, thankfully the rain had paused. Willy followed closely behind me as I walked along the slick gravel driveway leading to my front steps. Joanna must have heard us pull up because just as I was about to ring the bell, she was at the door greeting us with open arms and a loving smile. Maybe it was my imagination, maybe it was my guilty conscience, but somehow she looked amazingly younger since we'd been gone.

"Hey guys! Welcome home! How was it?"

"What a great experience," I answered, "Wish you could have been there! Arizona is freakin' gorgeous!"

I could read Willy's mind as I placed my luggage down in the hallway and needles of guilt punched holes in my heart.

"Well, I just wanted to say hello, Joanna," Willy said while quickly kissing her on the cheek, and then turning to me he added, "Maybe you guys want to get out for dinner tonight?"

"I'll call you," I said, as he scooted back towards the waiting limo as the sky politely held back the looming rain.

I closed the door behind Willy; Joanna looked at me tenderly and sighed, "I haven't seen you in two weeks! I don't want to go out with anyone tonight…I thought we'd spend the night alone!"

I felt like such a worthless dirty slug.

The Three Extras

John Rullo

~ RICH AND BARELY FAMOUS~

Ever since we'd first gone to California, Jack had mentioned, time and time again, how one day, if he had his way, he'd be living there. He fell in love with the San Diego beaches, the ideal weather and the laid back lifestyle. Unbeknownst to Willy and me, Jack had contacted a real estate agent to search out some properties. We had been making some pretty good money in our new career, so being able to afford the move was not even a question.

Tracy's parents were practically snowbirds. For quite a few years they've had a second home in West Palm Beach, Florida, and on several occasions, Willy, Tracy, Joanna and I spent some vacation time there. Joanna had so enjoyed our visits that she often suggested we buy a place of our own. My argument had always been we couldn't meet the expense of having two homes. As much as I loved spending a few cold winter weeks down south, I wasn't sure if I could live there year round. Willy, on the other hand, loved the southeast coast of Florida and when we used to sit in the lanai of his in-laws' place, just minutes from the beach, he used to dream of the four of us owning neighboring homes, taking walks along the shoreline and spending daily cocktail hours together. Money was no longer an issue. There was absolutely nothing stopping us from fulfilling some of these dreams and desires.

It was on a night about two months after we had returned from Arizona, when the six of us went out to dinner and Jack hit us with the bittersweet news. He and Jenny had put a bid on a place in San Diego and if everything went according to plan, they would be relocating. I was somewhat upset over hearing this because it was the first time since we met in high school we would be so far apart. Jack and Jenny were so excited about their prospective new home, and although I wanted to share in their joy, the thought of knowing he would soon be living over 2,000 miles away was distressing.

"What about the Three Extras?" I asked apprehensively, wondering if their move would somehow jeopardize our newfound success.

"John, Willy," he answered reassuringly, "Nothing will ever come between the three of us. When duty calls, I'll just have to meet you there! Aside from our working together, how often have we really gotten together since we've had families anyway?"

"It's just nice knowing you're close by," I whimpered like a kid who had just lost his best friend.

Jack's pending move to California lit a fire under Willy and me, so we began to do a little investigating of our own. Wendy Levine once happened to mention her sister was a real estate broker in Boca Raton. We decided to give her a call and in a matter of days she had e-mailed us an extensive list of luxurious houses for sale. We flew down to Florida with our wives and spent a week in the company of an extremely patient broker, who showed us at least thirty available homes. Due to the slump in the economy, property value in Florida had declined considerably, enabling Willy and I to place bids on side by side lavish waterfront homes in West Palm Beach. Joanna and Tracy were ecstatic to learn our bids were accepted and their dreams of owning Florida homes were soon to be a reality. The excitement of having new homes to decorate and furnish kept the girls preoccupied, so when we received a call from Wendy, who was bubbling with the good news of yet another road trip for the Three Extras, they took it a little better than usual.

It was a spring day of 2013 when the three of us were back in the offices of the Starlight Agency. *Tenders* was due for June release but news had leaked within the industry about the three interesting new magnetic faces that Scorsese had used in the film. Wendy's phone had been ringing off the hook with inquiries as to who we were and whether or not we were available to appear in soon-to-be-made movies by some of Hollywood's finest directors. Wendy's eyes were bulging, looking as if they were about to burst out of her head, because she couldn't hold back the exciting news any longer.

"Fellows, I don't quite understand what's going on, but it seems like the word is out on you guys! Tim Burton, Woody Allen, Ron Howard and Steven Spielberg want to schedule interviews!"

"I don't get it," a perplexed Willy responded, "We never say anything, we just stand or sit where they tell us, why is there suddenly such a demand for us? Anybody can do what we do!"

"This is a crazy business, there's no rhyme or reason. One day you're hot, the next day, you're not. All I can tell you, is when opportunity knocks, run with it! Obviously, Hollywood finds your mugs quite intriguing!"

Wendy didn't quite get it either, but as long as she was compensated quite well for acting as our agent, she was as happy as can be. As she flipped through the pile of papers on her cluttered desk, she spoke without looking up. "There's a new young director who contacted me regarding having you fellows appear in what will be his first major motion picture. It is a film with a working title of *River Rats* and his cast is made up of all virtually unknowns. The buzz going 'round is that the screenplay is brilliant and a major studio is giving this fellow a shot at directing it. His name is Alan Jordan and he was mentored by Mr. Scorsese. That's a pretty good credential, I would say!"

"Where are we headed to this time," I asked.

"If we can make this fit into your schedule, you're bound for Peru!" Wendy answered as her eyes peered heavenward, "I think somebody up there is looking after you guys."

"I've always wanted to visit South America," Jack said with a satisfied grin.

Everything seemed to be happening rather fast. Jack and Jenny's offer on the California house was accepted and they were anxious to move in. Joanna and Tracy were eager to get to Florida to begin making the new homes our own. In the meantime, Alan Jordan informed Wendy that if we agreed to do the movie he would need us on location where shooting would begin in two weeks. To complicate things even more, Ron Howard notified Wendy he was going to be in New York at the end of the month and wanted a meeting with us to discuss appearing in his upcoming black comedy, *Homeless in Hawaii*. Our retired lives had gradually transformed into a non-stop spiral of airports, hotels, limousines, and restaurants. We were bouncing back and forth between two residences, catering to our families, while trying to keep a career alive by hob-knobbing with celebrities and meeting with directors. Sometimes I was overwhelmed by the feeling we were about to take on more than we had bargained for.

Peru and the filming of *River Rats* was an adventure unlike anything I've ever imagined. Again we were cast in non-speaking roles, this time, as American tourists who just so happened to be in the wrong place at the wrong time. The plot took us on board a jungle cruise along the Amazon River where our boat gets seized by the pirates who dwell along its banks. A group, including Willy, Jack & me gets taken hostage and all we were basically expected to do was remain silent and act as though we were petrified, a task that was rather simple considering where we were.

    For me, experiencing the Amazon was like being lifted off the earth and transported to another time period. At any second I thought Tarzan was going to come swinging on a vine through the brush. The scenery was absolutely magnificent. I had never seen vegetation, plant life, insects, reptiles or animals anything like what was indigenous to that part of the earth. The bugs were the size of crows and I could sense the eyes of the creatures looming in the trees size us up. Every day began with coating ourselves from head to toe with insect repellent. We were actually able to witness the daily ritual in the lives of several jungle natives as we travelled along the river, and for the life of me, I couldn't believe how people lived so primitively in the twenty-first century. The tribes inhabiting the heart of the jungle were unacquainted with the modern conveniences of the nearby industrialized cities. There were no signs of plumbing or electricity. They fished and hunted for their food and cooked on open fires. They risked their lives each and every time they bathed in the river thick with caiman and piranha, never giving thought to cover themselves as their bare bodies wangled their way past hanging twisted vines, plodding along the dirt paths leading to their grass huts. It was steamy hot and very humid, my clothes felt like they were pasted to my body. Each day I couldn't wait for the shooting to end so I could get back to the rustic hotel in the village where I cooled off in the community shower and then stood naked in front of the one antiquated fan in my room.

Thank goodness our stay in Peru wasn't even two weeks. I don't think I could have taken a minute more. Willy wasn't enjoying himself very much, either, and he let us know it every chance he could, complaining, "What the fuck are we doing in the god-damned jungle when we have beautiful beach homes in Florida?"

"If it weren't for us doing these movies, my friend," I reminded him, "We wouldn't have those lovely homes in Florida!"

Jack was surprisingly very agreeable on that particular trip. He didn't complain about the heat, the bugs or the food. I attribute this to a relatively unknown actress named Veronica Pond. I was never very good at determining a woman's age, but I estimated her to be in her early thirties. She was stunning, yet she was a natural beauty. She had dark-blond, vibrant hair that sprung right into place with every step she took. Her cut-off safari shorts and tank top revealed almost all of her perfect, slender, bronze body. Her contagious smile, button nose and hypnotic gemstone-blue eyes had Jack helplessly trapped in her spell. Both Willy and I have had our turns at being captivated by beautiful women, but Jack, for as long as we'd known him, had been true blue, stuck to Jenny like glue and never even contemplated straying…at least until he met Miss Pond. Veronica seemed to have an eye for Jack, making it extremely difficult for him not to take notice of her. One afternoon she had asked him to apply sun block to her shoulders, and as he obliged her, we couldn't help but notice how his cheeks reddened and his brow broke out in a nervous sweat. There was definitely a battle going in Jack's conscience as flesh and spirit disagreed; his body language displaying how badly he wanted to devour her. Due to the circumstances, such as the uncomfortable heat and humidity, the very un-private accommodations at the hotel, and the rigid shooting schedule, Veronica's tempting passes failed to produce anything other than the groundwork for an attempted tryst in the future.

Being part of the making of *River Rats* was a rather unique experience for us. Everyone in the cast, including the director, was an unknown. We didn't have to deal with anyone being star-struck or intimidated by being in the presence of a world renowned celebrity because we were all more or less at the same level. Alan Jordan was very fortunate to have had the backing of a major studio and the financial support to make the film without the help of sure-fire big name box-office draws. From what I saw, the acting demonstrated by the new talent was incredible, and I knew some of the performances were certainly Oscar worthy. For the first time in our movie-making travels, however, I was happy and more than ready to return to the comforts of home. The conditions we had to endure in the heart of the jungle were practically intolerable. My arms and legs served as a banquet for the nibbling jungle insects that made me scratch until I drew blood. Before we eagerly departed the unpleasantries of the tropics, we made sure to say our good-byes to the cast members and crew. Alan thanked us for our cooperative efforts and mentioned, like all our directors had in the past, what a pleasure it had been to work with us. He guaranteed that we would be hearing from him for parts in his future films. As much as it delighted us to hear the good news, we agreed, if it meant having to return to the jungle, we were going to politely pass. I couldn't wait to get the hell out of there.

On the return flight, if Jack mentioned Veronica once, he mentioned her a thousand times. "That Veronica Pond was a beautiful woman, don't you think?" he asked matter-of-factly.

The Three Extras

"Yeah, she was pretty hot," I concurred, "Couldn't get your eyes off of her, could you?"

"Was it that obvious?" he asked.

"Obvious!" Willy blurted, "You looked like a wolf salivating over a baby lamb. Thought your heart was gonna explode while you were rubbing lotion on her shoulders!"

"Shit," Jack admitted, "I need to get laid!"

Instead of heading directly to our new homes to be with our wives, we had flown back to New York for another meeting with Wendy to review our itinerary, which included a meeting with Ron Howard the very next day. Although neither of us would openly admit it, our schedule was becoming exhausting. We loved the work and the money, but we felt as if we were taking on too much. Wendy kept reminding us opportunities like the ones we were having didn't come along every day and it would be in our best interest to jump at every offer. Of course, it was in Wendy's best interest as well!

Our calendar was jam packed. The conference with Ron Howard took place in Wendy's office where, after drowning him in accolades, we were asked to appear in his new film, *Homeless in Hawaii*. Ron was everything we thought he would be: friendly, unassuming, real down-to-earth, and funny. He appeared to be more uptight about meeting us than we were about meeting him. He was comfortably dressed in cargo shorts, denim work shirt with the sleeves rolled up, black slip-on canvas sneakers and, like Jack, the trademark cap that covered the absence of hair. Although the content of the film never mattered much to us, Mr. Howard was very excited about the project and took the opportunity to passionately explain the plot.

"The story is centered on the life of an unfulfilled Manhattan businessman who is not appreciated by the company to which he gave his blood, sweat and tears or the family for which he worked so hard to support. One night after work, as he was walking towards the subway, he encounters a homeless man who hits him up for a couple bucks. Instead of feeling sorry for the beggar, he envisions himself as a homeless man escaping his mundane, monotonous, unsatisfied, unacknowledged existence. He decides that if one is to consciously make the decision to be homeless, why do it in a dirty city?" Ron paused for a moment, and after assuming from our enthusiastic smiles we approved, he eagerly continued. "He then leaves everything to his selfish, undeserving family and buys a one-way ticket to Hawaii figuring if he's going to be homeless, why not be homeless in a beautiful place? While there, he learns to survive on coconuts and the generosity of tourists. Great concept, don't you think?"

Wendy, Jack, Willy and I shared in his exuberance as he went on to inform us that movie was going to be shot on location in New York City and Hawaii.

"I think you fellows are going to be perfect," Ron said enthusiastically, "I sincerely hope you will allow me the opportunity to include your charming faces in my film!"

"Thanks, Mr. Howard," Willy humbly replied, "But I keep wanting to call you Opie!"

Wendy, a little embarrassed by Willy's remark, laughed and said, "How many times have you heard someone say that, Ron!"

Sensing Wendy's awkwardness, he answered, "Actually no one has ever said that to me before!"

Everyone had a laugh, Ron presented us with tentative schedules, and Wendy promised to keep in close contact. We all shook hands with Opie and just before leaving the office, Jack asked one last question.

"Is there any chance of letting us in on who will be starring in the film, Ron?"

"Oh, I'm sorry," he said, while hitting himself on the side of his head, "How did I forget to mention that? Owen Wilson has agreed to take on the lead role and a newcomer by the name of Veronica Pond will be co-starring."

Jack couldn't believe his ears when he heard the name Veronica Pond. We could actually feel the vibes radiating from his body as his throat suddenly seemed to tighten and his voice went up an octave.

"Oh," Jack practically squealed with joyful anxiety, "I, uh, really like Owen Wilson!"

Willy and I flew down to Florida where we joined up with our wives, only to get right back on a plane with them a few days later and head out together to Hollywood for the world premier of *Tenders*. At the same time, Jack was on board a California-bound jet to meet Jenny at their new home in San Diego. The six of us connected the following day at the Universal Theater in LA where we mingled among all the VIPS who were invited to attend the screening of our very first major motion picture. What a thrill it was to see the many promotional movie posters displayed about the premises with Jack, Willy and me posed in scenes with the stars, Marisa Tomei, Jeff Bridges, James Franco and Keanu Reeves. When Martin Scorsese arrived, he recognized us immediately and rushed through the crowd in order to greet us.

"Hey fellows," he said happily, "So good to see you again."

"Likewise, Mr. Scorsese," answered Jack, and pointing to our wives, he continued, "These are our lovely wives Joanna, Tracy and Jenny…"

"The pleasure is all mine ladies, and please, call me Marty! Your husbands are naturals; what took them so long to get into show business? I think you're going to like what you're about to see!"

"I'm sure we will, Mr. Scor...uh, I mean, Marty!" Jenny said in between nervous giggles.

Just as Marty excused himself to circulate among the other guests, Marisa Tomei came casually strolling into the theater lobby, and as if she were equipped with a tracking device, immediately spotted Willy.

"Willy," she called out in a high-pitched bubbly voice all her own, "So good to see you, sweetie!" Acknowledging Jack, me and the three ladies by our sides, she resumed, "Hey, guys, aren't you going to introduce me to your friends?"

I don't think Willy ever stopped to consider that the chances were pretty good he'd be running into Marisa. With Tracy attached to his hip all night, it was an especially awkward moment when Marisa grabbed Willy's hand, pulled him close and greeted him with a overly friendly kiss. His nervousness was easily detectable as he introduced Tracy to Marisa with a stutter, "This is, uh, my, uh, my uh, my wife, Tr...Tr...Tracy, Ma, Ma, Marisa!"

"Good to meet you, Tracy; You've got a good man here!"

"So he tells me," Tracy said lightheartedly, "So he tells me!"

"Oh my God," Jenny whispered to Joanna, "I can't believe we're talking to Marisa Tomei!"

As Marisa got swept up into the crowd, she stood on her tip toes and cried out, "Let's meet up after the movie!" and then blended into the vivacious gathering of celebrities and wannabes.

"A little bit too friendly, wouldn't you say?" Tracy quivered with a tinge of suspicion.

The Three Extras

"Oh that's just the way she is with everybody," Willy insisted, "She makes me nervous!"

Tracy didn't pursue the argument, put aside her suspicions, and the six of us proceeded to take our seats as the movie was about to begin. Jenny was antsy, turning her head each and every way hoping to get a glimpse of a movie star. "Oh my God," she blurted with uncontainable excitement, "There's Keanu Reeves and Jeff Bridges."

Jack, who was embarrassed by her star-struck behavior, pulled her by the arm and pleaded, "Please Jen, for the next few hours how about pretending you're one of them!"

Although we didn't have any clue of what to expect, we knew it was going to be quite a thrill for us to finally see our faces on the same screen with famous Hollywood actors and actresses. The six of us sat anxiously anticipating our big moment and when it arrived, Jack, Willy and I got solid elbow jabs to the side from our overly excited, proud spouses.

"How cool is this," Tracy whispered, restraining herself from cheering wildly.

"You guys look so great!" Joanna admitted softly, joyfully surprised at the results of our long stretch of desertion from home.

We had no idea what the amount of our actual screen time would be or who we would even be seen with. Many of the scenes we remembered shooting were obviously scratched; in fact, none of the footage from LA made it to the final print. A little disappointed that we only appeared in a few of the New York scenes taken at Shemp's Tavern, it was still very exciting being even a small part of a Scorsese film.

Even though our Hollywood debut showed no real signs of acting ability, it was a proud moment and in the eyes of our wives we were stars. The first showing culminated with thunderous applause from the satisfied audience and as we patiently tried to maneuver our way through the theater lobby and out to the street, we were recognized by critics, paparazzi and movie fans who congratulated us as if we had starring roles. For the first time since our post mid-life show biz career began, I was overwhelmed. It was like living a dream. We were nobodies, yet we were being treated as if we weren't. Willy thought for the sake of his marriage it would be best if he didn't have to face Marisa again, so we forfeited any ideas we had of attending the after parties. We obliged his wishes, much to Jenny's disappointment. Unlike her, Joanna and Tracy weren't star struck or very easily impressed; they could not have cared less and preferred we would just keep to ourselves.

"They're just people," Tracy reminded her friend, "They piss, shit and vomit just like we do!"

"It feels like high school and college all over again," Jack noted as we quietly slipped into the fully stocked limousine he arranged to have waiting for us, which took us on the two and a half hour drive to his new San Diego home.

"I don't recall getting picked up by fancy cars when we were in high school," Willy said with a chuckle.

"You know what I mean," Jack answered. "Being with you guys and having this popularity; I'm just fondly remembering those good old times."

In unison we called out, "To us!"

Rather than hightailing it back and forth from Florida and New York and then over to California again, Willy, Tracy, Joanna and I decided to spend a few days with Jack and Jenny in sunny southern California before the Three Extras had to leave for Hawaii. The Reilly's new spread was a spacious ultra modern condominium in a luxurious high security development walking distance from the beach. While Jenny took Tracy and Joanna for a late night tour of her new home, Jack, Willy and I made ourselves comfortable on the newly arrived living room furniture.

"I can't believe the three of us are sitting here in your San Diego condo and in just two days we'll be in Hawaii making a movie with Ron-fucking-Howard?" Willy pondered aloud.

"Why couldn't this have happened to us thirty years ago?" I questioned.

"Because everything is timing," Jack answered with the wisdom of an old professor, "The world wasn't ready for us then and who knows, we may not have been able to handle it!"

The next forty-eight hours were reminiscent of the old days when the six of us were inseparable. We spent time at the beach, ate at nice restaurants and hung out at Jack and Jenny's, drinking and chatting to all hours of the morning, the way we used to when they first got married. Sitting on their balcony, sipping a remarkable Napa Valley red blend, gazing up at the luster of the full moon suspended above the Pacific, each of us was overpowered by the unexplainable sensation we were being looked after. We realized how blessed we were to have had remained friends for so many years. I was having such a pleasant time just relaxing and reliving moments from our youth, I was no longer over-enthused about schlepping to yet another airport. Joanna and Tracy stayed with Jenny in San Diego for a few more days before they returned home to Florida. Jack, Willy and I were headed off to Maui, where for two weeks we would be in the company of Ron Howard, Owen Wilson, Veronica Pond, and the rest of the cast and crew of *Homeless in Hawaii*. We tried to persuade the girls to join us on our Hawaiian adventure but they were anxious to add the finishing touches to their new residences. Besides, after once having a taste of accompanying us on the road only to be ignored and bored out of their minds, they chose to never travel with us to a movie shoot ever again.

We arrived late Monday afternoon, and as it was with every production we had been associated with, rooms were reserved for us at one of the finest hotels. The clerk at the desk in the main lobby presented us with a letter that had been left by our director with instructions for us to meet at the nearby Pineapple Grill for dinner.

"Sometimes I get the feeling somebody is playing a very expensive joke on us," Willy said as we approached the entrance to the restaurant, "Movie extras just don't get the treatment we've been getting. Something about all this just feels strange."

"You're just realizing this now?" I asked.

"Never question good fortune," Jack advised, "Just go with it!"

When we walked into The Pineapple Grill, we were greeted with the most engaging smile from a captivatingly beautiful Hawaiian hostess, clad in the stereotypical grass skirt and bikini top.

"Welcome to the Pineapple Grill, will you be three for dinner?"

"Ah, yes," Jack replied, "We were instructed to ask for Mr. Howard's party…"

"Oh!" she exclaimed with delight, "You must be the Three Extras! So nice to meet you, follow me!"

"I'm telling you," Willy repeated, "This is too fucking weird!"

We followed our hostess to a table in the corner where Ron Howard leaped to his feet the moment he noticed us.

"John, Jack, Willy! So good to see you!" he said as he firmly and enthusiastically shook each of our hands.

The Three Extras

"Good to see you again," Jack replied in his usual spokesman manner.

Sitting alongside Mr. Howard were two unfamiliar faces, a woman who I estimated was probably in her mid-forties and a younger man who I guessed to be no older than thirty-five. Pointing to the woman, Ron said, "This is Evelyn, my personal assistant. If you fellows ever encounter a problem or have any questions, please feel free to approach her." Evelyn, petite and rather plain-faced, raised her glass, smiled and nodded in approval. Directing his attention to the man, he continued, "And this is Jason. Most of your scenes are going to be shot on the beach. Whenever any of you feel the need to get out of the sun, wash up, want something to drink, or relax between scenes, Jason will be on hand to direct you to your trailer and see to it you are accommodated." Jason, appearing more like a high school nerd than a director's assistant, imitated Evelyn by raising his glass, smiling and nodding in approval. From behind his trademark smile, Mr. Howard then proceeded to explain our non-speaking roles as American tourists, "The extent of your obligations," he stated, "Will be to lie on the beach, sit at the bar, and dine in a restaurant."

"We can do that," I replied snappily, "We're retirees!"

We ordered drinks with umbrellas in them and shortly after toasting to the movie's success, Owen Wilson and Veronica Pond joined our little group. Jack's assertive personality abruptly changed to one of passive vulnerability the second his eyes met Veronica's. Immediately, the atmosphere around our table changed as Jack's confidence seemed threatened.

"So nice to see you boys again," she purred, her eyes never once deserting Jack.

"So you all know each other," Owen inquired.

With her eyes glued to Jack, Veronica made no attempt to downplay her very obvious fixation. "Yeah, Owen," I answered, "We met in Peru on the set of *River Rats*."

"I understand that's supposed to be a tremendous movie," Evelyn added to the conversation, detecting the instantly recognizable sexual energy between Jack and Ms. Pond.

"That's what we hear," Willy mumbled after taking a sip of his Grand Marnier cocktail, "All I know is I couldn't wait to get the hell off of that set! I was covered in bug bites!"

It was evident Veronica couldn't wait to pick up where she and Jack had left off in South America and it was also noticeable how Jack preferred not to be in such a vulnerable situation, that is, in Hawaii, miles away from Jenny with a voluptuous woman who couldn't wait to jump his bones.

"Well, what do you say we get a good night's sleep," Jack suggested to Willy and me seeking some support. "We've got a busy week ahead of us!"

"Good idea," Ron Howard eagerly agreed, "I think we about covered everything."

As we all rose from the table, with her sights set on Jack, Veronica sighed, "The night's still young; does anyone care to join me for a nightcap?"

"Uh...I would actually love to," Jack trembled as he spoke, "but I can hear my pillow calling my name."

"Well then perhaps another time, handsome," she pouted disappointedly while making sure to lightly brush her body against his as she walked past him.

The first day of shooting was Wednesday and we reported for duty on the beach promptly at six AM. Jason was there to direct us to our assigned trailer and make sure we were

The Three Extras

comfortable. "Whatever you need, I'm at your disposal," he cheerfully reminded us. Many of our initial scenes didn't require any interacting with the lead characters. We simply wore what we were told to wear, stood where we told to stand, lay where we were told to lie, and sat where we were told to sit. It was, without a doubt, the easiest work we were ever asked to do. Even though the days were extremely long and tedious, who had it better than us? Maui was heaven on earth. The air was fresh and energizing, the water a serene crystal blue, the food fresh and plentiful, and the beaches pristine. At times I felt guilty not being able to share it all with Joanna.

One of the many perks of being involved in the making of a major motion picture was the exquisite catering. From what we've been able to conclude, actors and actresses are a demanding bunch with sophisticated, hard to please palates. On every set of our short career, gourmet foods were always plentiful. Our stay in Hawaii, however, allowed us to sample exotic cuisine unlike anything we'd ever seen. I'd always been a very finicky eater, very selective about what I choose to swallow. Willy and Jack, on the other hand, would bravely try anything at least once. During our stay in paradise, I was astonished by some of the squiggly, slimy taste treats my two best friends dared to ingest.

The week flew by, and before we knew it, what was scheduled to be our last day of soaking up the Maui sunshine was upon us. Our scenes were all in the can, as they say in the business, and Mr. Howard, no different than the other directors we'd worked with, commended us on doing a fine job, although we weren't even sure what we did, other than to get pampered and enjoy the heavenly sights of this remarkably beautiful island. A huge spread of assorted Hawaiian delicacies, including squid luau, poke, Okinawan pig's feet soup and Spam musubi had been made available to the cast and crew members, and Jack was quite adventurous in trying all but one dish. I couldn't say for sure what it was, but it seemed like a rare variety of sea creature, closely resembling human organs, in a pool of purplish sauce. After courageously trying some of the mysterious yet delicious provisions, the three of us returned to our trailer in order to gather our belongings and then head back to the hotel where we were planning to wind down before the long flight home. It hadn't even been a minute after we stepped foot inside, when we heard four quick knocks on our trailer door. The door swung open and in strutted none other than Veronica Pond. Barefoot and casually dressed in a loose-fitting grey tank top and snug white Capri pants, her eyes zeroed in on Jack like a hawk zooming in on its prey. Almost as if Willy and I weren't in the room, she walked right up to him and asked in a sultry Marilyn Monroe sigh, "Were you going to leave the island without saying goodbye?"

Adjusting the rim of his ever-present baseball cap, Jack answered with nervous hesitation, "Of course not Veronica, just getting some things together...uh, what made you think we wouldn't say goodbye?"

Without turning her gaze from Jack for even a second, her next comment was directed towards me and Willy, "Could you boys excuse us for a few minutes? I have a few things I'd like to discuss with your partner!"

Willy and I shrugged our shoulders and stood dumbfounded, wondering why in the world this beautiful starlet had such an obsession for Jack. Then again, we wondered what in the world Hollywood saw in the three of us! Jack knew for certain if he was left alone with her he'd succumb, so combining ingenuity with quick thinking, he bent over to reach for his sandals and from his crouching position said, "it's okay Veronica, anything you have to tell me you can tell my friends!"

"I wouldn't feel comfortable," she replied, "you can tell them yourself later if you choose to," as she pointed towards the door and positioned herself in such a way that when Jack stood, his face would meet up squarely between her long slender legs.

We knew there was no way Veronica was going to allow Jack to escape whatever it was she had in mind, so we did what good friends do; we left him alone with her.

"If you need us, we'll be on the beach," I reassured him jokingly, "see you in a bit!"

As Willy and I clumsily stepped out of the trailer, she said "Thank you, men! I'm sure your friend will appreciate it!" and gently kicked the door shut behind us.

"She's going to eat him alive!" Willy remarked.

"Not for anything," I added, "but I'd love to be a fly on the trailer wall right now. I thought for sure she was gonna devour him when they met in Peru! I hope his heart can take it!"

"Don't even say that," Willy chuckled, "that's all we need right now!"

"Obviously, he must have something she wants!"

"Obviously," Willy agreed.

Proving once again that great minds think alike, simultaneously we pronounced, "I know she sure has something I want!"

We could not deny she was certainly a strikingly beautiful woman.

As Willy and I walked along the beach, consciously making the effort not to venture too far off, we recalled how during our two week stay in Maui, Veronica coincidentally seemed to be everywhere we were; the restaurants, the bars, the beach, and the pool. It suddenly struck us that she had been stalking Jack, tracking his whereabouts until she finally got him where she wanted him. We were getting a good laugh trying to imagine what may have been going on in that trailer. "You think he keeps his hat on when he's getting laid," Willy asked, laughing hysterically at his own question. Before I could answer, we heard a shrill scream coming from the direction we had just left moments ago. We saw the door of our trailer bust open and Veronica come running out wearing nothing but panties. She appeared to be in a state of panic, signaling for help.

"Oh my God," she cried, "call an ambulance! Get help!"

Willy and I ran back to the trailer as fast as we could, kicking up enough sand to create a whiteout. We arrived in a matter of minutes and found a bare-chested Jack with his pants down around his ankles. He was as white as a ghost, his face grimacing with pain, laid out on the futon with his hands holding his chest. In spite of our worry for Jack, we could not help noticing, much to our pleasure, Veronica bent over to pick her clothes up from the floor and much to our dismay, she got dressed!

"Easy Jack," I said calmly, "you're gonna be alright!"

"You had to go and jinx him, didn't you," Willy panicked, as if my mentioning the possibility of his heart giving out had anything to do with what was happening.

"Johnny, I've got such a sharp pain in my chest…Christ, if Jenny finds out about this…"

"Nobody's going to know anything and we're going to get you right to a hospital!" Willy and I gently pulled up Jack's pants and covered his chest with his shirt. Within minutes, a group of folks including Evelyn, Jason, Owen and Ron had gathered at our trailer, Jason reassuring us that an ambulance was on the way.

"I'm so sorry," Veronica cried, "He didn't tell me he had a weak heart!"

"What do you want us to do, Jack," Willy questioned, "do we call Jenny?"

"He never told me he was married," Veronica sighed, "Oh my goodness, what did we go and do?"

"No! Not yet," Jack insisted with a labored whisper, "Let's wait!"

The ambulance arrived. Two medics took Jack's vitals and then carefully placed him onto a stretcher and into the back of the vehicle. Veronica and I crammed into the back of the ambulance with Jack and one of the medics, while Willy rode in the front passenger seat.

"I think it's my heart," Jack moaned, "What am I gonna tell Jen? I'm gonna have to call her, she's expecting me home tonight, in fact, she's planning on picking me up at the airport!"

"Relax, my friend, don't worry," I said reassuringly, although none of us we're thinking straight at the time, "We'll figure out how to deal with Jenny."

"I feel terrible," sighed a much shaken Veronica, "why didn't he tell me he had a heart condition…I could have killed him!"

"Yeah," I kidded, "but what a way to go!"

"Thanks a lot," Jack grumbled, his hands still resting upon his chest.

"I assume you're not his wife," the medic questioned Veronica while checking Jack's pulse. The medic was a handsome young man, probably in his early thirties. Surprisingly, he wasn't a native Hawaiian. His name was Adam, a Jewish fellow who had relocated from Syosset, Long Island. He was wearing blue hospital scrubs, his V-neck top revealing just a hint of his muscular chest where a gold surfboard dangled from a chain. His long black hair was combed straight back and except for the one strand that drooped down onto his sun-bronzed face, always in perfect place. He had one eye on Jack who was taking slow and laborious deep breaths and one eye studying Veronica's striking body. Without once letting her out of his sight, he removed Jack's shirt and carefully applied all the contacts and wires necessary for an EKG.

"He's a colleague," she answered, "Is he going to be alright?"

"Let's hope so," he said dryly, as if he'd been through the routine hundreds of times before.

When we arrived at the hospital, Jack was taken directly to the emergency room where they conducted immediate tests to determine whether or not he did have another heart attack. Willy, Veronica and I sat in the waiting room pondering what our next move should be.

"I guess first we had better reschedule our flights," Willy suggested, "and then we need to call Jenny and the girls!"

"What do we say?" I asked, "We can't tell them the truth!"

As Willy and I tried to concoct a story, Adam and his partner casually sauntered through the waiting room pushing the stretcher they had carried Jack in upon earlier.

"You go on ahead," Adam told his co-worker, "I'll be there in a minute!"

He walked over to where we were seated and tried to show some concern by saying, "I hope your friend is going to be alright." He then displayed his real intentions when he handed a business card to Veronica making her an offer loaded with ulterior motives, "If ever you decide you may want surfing lessons, look me up! It's been a pleasure meeting you."

"Thanks, I'll keep it in mind," she replied distractedly, folding the card and tucking it into the waist band of her pocketless pants. Adam walked off, turning his head every few feet to gawk at her until he disappeared through the exit doors.

"Wow," I said, "Could he have been any more obvious?"

"Handsome, but creepy," Veronica noted as she retrieved the card, tore it in two and placed it in the trash.

"Can you answer me a question, Veronica?" Willy requested.

"Sure," she obliged.

"What is it that you see in Jack?"

Veronica smiled and answered affectionately, "He's got the most adorable face for an older man and I find him extremely sexy!"

"You know," Willy informed her, "For as long as we've known him, he's never been unfaithful to Jenny."

"Maybe he's just never met anybody worth cheating with," she spoke confidently, "And not once did he ever mention he was married…none of you guys have that married look!"

"Oh, we're married alright!" I reminded her, "And how we're going to get him out of this jam, I don't know!"

Willy called Wendy at her New York office and asked her to please cancel our flight reservations. Without giving away all the details, he simply explained Jack was undergoing a slight medical problem and would elaborate when we knew more. Too bad I didn't keep it that simple when I had called Joanna and informed her we were going to be detained in Hawaii because Jack was taken to the hospital due to a sudden health issue. Joanna pressed for details. I had the ball and I fumbled, which needlessly aroused her suspicion.

"Health issue?" she asked curiously, "What kind of health issue?"

"Uh, we're at the hospital now, babe. Waiting to hear from the doctors," I said.

"Yeah, I get that, but what happened? Was it his stomach, his heart? Did he break something, pass out?"

"He got some pains in his chest," I answered without getting specific.

"Just like that?" she probed, "What was he doing?"

"How the hell am I supposed to know?" I snapped, feeling the stress of possibly saying the wrong thing, "Suddenly he didn't look so good, uh, and said he was feeling, uh, chest pains…"

"Did anybody contact Jenny?"

"Uh, yeah, Willy, uh, called Jen…"

"I'll call you as soon as we learn anything…love you!"

Telling Joanna that Willy contacted Jenny was a big mistake. I should have been firm in stating how Jack didn't want to worry Jen until they knew what was wrong, but under pressure, I didn't take the time to think things out. Two seconds after I had hung up on my probing wife, she called Jen to see if there was anything she could do. Jenny had no idea what Joanna was talking about. When my cell phone rang and I saw Jenny's name appear on the caller ID, I knew there was going to be trouble. Brave soul I was, I didn't answer figuring she would leave a voice message, which she did. I couldn't tell if she sounded confused, furious, or both. "John Colletti, what the fuck is going on. Is Jack alright? I just got off the phone with Joanna and something's not kosher…Are you three hiding something from me? Call me back as soon as you get this!"

Willy saw the troubled look on my face and asked what was wrong. Just as I was about to tell him, his cell phone rang and looking at the caller ID he said, "It's Jenny!"

"Don't answer it!" I commanded abruptly and explained what had just happened.

"Shit," Willy sighed in exasperation, "Now what? I'm telling you, woman fucking know when something's up!"

At that moment, Joanna had called again demanding answers. "What the hell are you guys hiding? Are the three of you screwing around?"

"Joanna!" I whined, "How could you think such a thing?"

"If it was anything other than what we suspect, why wouldn't someone have called Jenny?"

"What do you mean by 'we suspect?'"

"What do you think, Jenny's stupid? Why don't you just tell me what the fuck happened?"

Feeling cornered, I did my best to delicately explain how Veronica was irresistible and how she had been determined to seduce Jack since they first met in Peru. I also tried to persuade her into rationalizing that since it was his first offense, the only time since I've known Jack he has ever even considered messing around with another woman, that Jenny should go easy on him. Not buying my plea bargaining and not feeling at all sorry for him, Joanna said, "You're an asshole! That's what he gets for screwing around!" I only hoped and prayed no one would ever spill the beans about what happened in Sedona!

In the meantime, Jenny and Joanna had called Tracy, Tracy had called Willy and everyone, including Veronica, had presumed Jack had a heart attack in the middle of his first and only extramarital fling. Willy and I decided it would be best if we tried to put Jenny's mind at ease by fabricating some kind of story explaining the cause of Jack's sudden ailment. Willy called first, and as luck would have it, Jenny didn't answer. Willy left a lengthy lie on Jen's voice mail over-exaggerating an All-You-

Can-Eat Buffet Breakfast ingested by Jack that would make anybody believe it produced the symptoms of a heart attack. I called about ten minutes after Willy, hoping to leave a similar message, but wasn't as lucky. Jenny answered.

"Hey Jen," I said, trying to sound positive and credible, "It's been so crazy here. Jack really frightened us there for a minute. At first we thought it was from over-exerting himself in the ocean, but then we figured it was from what he ate for breakfast. We're waiting for the doctor's..."

"Save your bullshit, John Colletti. I know what happened. Someone from the ER called the house for insurance information and they had me speak to Jack. He was with a fucking woman and they're checking to see if he had a heart attack. He told me everything. You fucking guys are too much...always covering up for each other!"

"I'm sorry Jen..."

"Save it, John, and tell Willy he's a shitty liar. He can't even lie convincingly in a voice message. You guys suck!"

Feeling like three dirt bags, Willy and I sat beside Veronica in the crowded waiting room, impatiently killing time until we got an update on Jack's condition.

"Shit," Willy whined like a little boy who just got caught lying to his mother, "Now what?"

I shook my head and answered, "I don't know. Somehow we'll figure it out."

Veronica tried to ease our worried minds when she naively suggested, "Do you want me to talk to her?"

"Yeah right," I laughed, "That'll work!"

After what seemed like an eternal wait, a doctor in blue scrubs, appearing too young to even have a driver's license, entered the waiting room. "John Colletti," he called out while scanning the area looking for a responder. The three of us jumped to our feet and I raised my hand like a grade school student hoping to be called upon. The baby-faced doctor, clipboard in hand, was wearing a grin that made it seem like he was holding back from laughing out loud. His carefree manner suggested to us the news was going to be good. He reached out to shake my hand and introduced himself.

"Hello, I'm Dr. Kalua. Your friend is going to be alright. He will be out in a few more minutes."

"What was wrong, Doctor?" I asked, feeling somewhat relieved that his response wouldn't include the words 'heart attack.'

"Mr. Reilly suffered from a very bad case of gastritis. Something he ate most certainly didn't agree with him and brought on those severe chest pains. He's fine. Just make sure he eats light for the next 24 hours."

"Geez," Veronica moaned with a trace of disappointment in her voice, "Here I thought I gave the guy a heart attack and all he had was gas?"

"For Christ's sake Veronica," Willy exploded, "It's not about you. Jenny knows, Jack is screwed and she's never going to trust him or us again! Maybe if he had gotten laid it would have at least been worth all this trouble!"

"But since nothing happened," Veronica insisted, pleading her innocence, "His wife has no reason to hold it against him. It was the Kona coffee, the bacon, the shrimp and that Hawaiian buffet that did him in, not me!"

Just then, Jack pushed his way through the swinging doors that separated the examining quarters from the waiting room. Looking equally embarrassed and relieved to know it was his stomach and not his heart that landed him in the ER, Jack approached the three of us and said in a take-charge voice, "Let's get the hell out of here!" Veronica reached out and gently held on to Jack's hand. "I'm sorry," she said, then kissed him softly on the cheek.

"You're sorry!" Jack replied as the four of us marched through the exit doors and into the glow of the late afternoon Hawaiian sunlight.

Awkward was a mild way of describing how Willy, Jack and I felt when Jenny met us at the airport. Although he'd been accustomed to limousine service, Jenny was resolute about picking up her "in the dog house" husband. Originally, Willy and I weren't planning on spending any time in San Diego. We missed our wives and couldn't wait to meet up with them in our new Florida homes. Jack, however, had different plans for us and insisted we hung around as moral support, at least for a day.

Although Jenny appeared to be cordial, I could tell she was fuming on the inside, especially because of the unexpected presence of her spouse's two accessories. Throughout most of the ride she was silent, staring straight ahead while nervously tapping her fingers on the steering wheel in a quick steady rhythm, somehow controlling her temper and restraining herself from giving Jack the tongue lashing she thought he rightfully deserved. It wasn't until minutes before pulling into the entrance of their development when she couldn't hold back any longer, "What the fuck were you thinking? How can I ever trust you?"

Jack hesitated a few seconds before answering calmly, "Nothing happened, Jenny, nothing!"

"That's only because you thought you were having a fucking heart attack," she said slamming the dashboard.

"No it's not," Jack shot out in defense, "I was just about to ask her to leave when I got the pains in my chest…you know I would never…"

The Three Extras

Willy and I sat uncomfortably silent in the back seat pretending not to listen while Jack and Jenny argued. Both of us knew very well if Jenny didn't eventually believe Jack, or at least forgive him, this could be the end of the Three Extras.

"I swear to you Jenny," I insisted firmly, "Nothing happened. Jack did everything he could to avoid her."

"Oh yeah, John Colletti, like I'm supposed to take anything you have to say as credible. One of you scumbags lie and the other two swear to it! How many women have you two been screwing?" Turning her attention back to Jack, she asked, "What did you go and do asshole, ask your lying friends to come home with you and defend your bullshit story?"

Jenny pulled into the driveway, exited the car, slammed the door and made her way into the house. As the three of us reached for our luggage from the rear of the car, Willy suggested that maybe he and I ought to stay in a motel. Jack wouldn't hear of it and demanded we come in. After carefully placing down our suitcases in the foyer, we reluctantly made our way into the kitchen area where Jen had poured herself a generous glass of red wine.

"Are you going to offer me some?" I asked hesitantly.

"I hope you choke on it!" she said, the tightness in her throat making her words barely audible.

"Oh you don't mean that Jen," I replied lovingly, "We know each other too long and love each other too much."

Jenny took three wine glasses from the cabinet, slammed the bottle down on the granite counter and ordered us to help ourselves. "There's plenty more where this came from," she informed us, "I think we're going to need it!"

The four of us sat up until sunrise. We went through six bottles of wine and by the time we were ready to crash, all was forgiven. Willy and I swore up and down, right hand to God that

Jack was innocent, reviewing the details of our well rehearsed and almost true story over and over again. Jack actually shed a few real tears while begging for Jenny's forgiveness, going as far to mention even giving up his career as an extra, words Willy and I didn't want to believe we were hearing. I didn't know if it was solely because she was soused, but Jenny forgave us all and then openly declared her undying love for her husband. "Excuse us," she slurred while pulling Jack's arm, "We have some make-up sex to get to," and then the two of them disappeared down the hallway and into the master bedroom leaving Willy and I on our own.

"Well, well," Willy muttered through a silly smile and bloodshot eyes, "Our job is done here!" We stumbled up the stairs to our guest rooms, bid each other good night and slept soundly for the next twelve hours. The following day we miraculously awoke without hangovers to find Jack and Jenny in reasonably good spirits radiant in the afterglow of last night's make-up sex. It was just like old times when later in the day the four of us went out to dinner at a trendy waterfront restaurant and shared quite a few good laughs over the recent events. We watched as the California sun set into the Pacific and we toasted our lifelong friendship with a round of an outstanding thirty year brandy. No sooner than I laid my head on the pillow that very evening, the next morning arrived. Our hosts were already awake, the coffee was made, and after a round of heartfelt hugs, kisses and goodbyes, we were on our way to the airport to board a jet bound for West Palm Beach where we would soon be reunited with Joanna and Tracy.

The Three Extras

John Rullo

~WARNING SIGN ~

As much fun and excitement we may have been having while living in the shadows of the biggest names in Hollywood, sometimes it was just good to be at home relaxing. The girls did an outstanding job putting all the finishing touches on our new digs and amazingly, neither one of them raised any questions about the Veronica Pond fiasco with Jack. Home cooked meals and our own beds were a welcome change from the many restaurants and hotel rooms that had become part of our lives, and it seemed that Joanna and Tracy were unusually happy having us around. It appeared as though they had everything under control and couldn't do enough to please us.

On an absolutely perfect mid-January Sunday afternoon, the air was comfortable, relatively dry and the temperature was in the mid 70's, Joanna and I were hanging out next door with the Taylors. Willy and I were sitting beside the pool sipping bourbon on ice while the girls were inside preparing a salad and marinating salmon and vegetables for the grill. We were truly enjoying the comforts of home while sharing thoughts on the future of our movie career.

"So, where do you think we're headed next?" Willy wondered.

"I don't know my friend, but every day I smack myself to make sure I'm not dreaming!" Pointing to both our beautiful homes and the magnificent view of the Atlantic Ocean in the foreground, I continued, "How is it we got so lucky?"

The Three Extras

Just as Willy and I held our glasses high to toast our good fortune, Joanna let out a shrill scream from the kitchen window, "Willy…come quick…hurry!"

Immediately, Willy's Florida tan turned ghostly white. With no idea of what could have possibly been wrong, we dropped our drinks and dashed towards the house as fast as we could. Bursting into the kitchen, we saw Tracy's pale body quivering on the brown ceramic tile floor. She was in the fetal position, moaning and holding her stomach.

"Trace!" Willy shouted, his fear-filled eyes teeming with tears, as he fell to his knees beside her. "What's wrong?" he pleaded for an answer, "What's wrong?"

Tracy was grimacing with agony as she struggled to get out the words, "Call 911, my abdomen…cramping."

Willy didn't leave Tracy's side, his trembling hands caressing her brow and reaching for her fingers. I was trying my best to keep Willy calm, my hands upon his shoulders, assuring him that everything was going to be alright while Joanna was on the phone with 911.

Within minutes, two baby-faced EMT's leaped out of the ambulance that had pulled into Willy's driveway. One was a male, the other a female and neither of them could have been a day older than twenty-five. I led them into the house through the garage and as the girl immediately tended to Tracy, taking her vitals and asking where the pain was, the fellow kept staring at Willy and me until in a moment of revelation he snapped his fingers and said, "I know you! You're the guys in the TV commercial!"

"Are you fuckin' kidding me?" Willy snapped, "Aren't you supposed to be taking care of my wife?"

As an EMT in Florida, I'm sure the overawed fellow was so used to responding to the monotonous calls of feeble senior citizens, recognizing us came as an unexpected thrill. "I'm sorry, sir," he said as his face reddened, kneeling down beside his partner to check on Tracy.

The two young technicians gently moved Tracy onto a stretcher. Carefully they maneuvered her out of the house and into the rear of the ambulance. Tracy scowled with discomfort while Willy, trying unsuccessfully to mask his fear and keep his composure, looked as if his whole world had just collapsed. He hastily scrambled about the kitchen looking for his house keys and wallet, and then made sure the oven was turned off. His sallow complexion displayed his worry as he climbed into the front seat of the ambulance. Joanna and I scooted next door, hopped into our car and followed closely behind as the ambulance sped along to nearby Good Samaritan Hospital.

Joanna and I patiently sat in the waiting room eager for news on Tracy's condition. I was about to mention to her how it hadn't been very long since Willy and I were sitting outside a hospital emergency room awaiting the prognosis on Jack, but didn't want to open a can of worms. There wasn't much we could say to each other we didn't already say on the ride over, so we just sat and stared blindly into a television. A sudden jab to the arm from Joanna's elbow shook me out from my trance. "Oh my God," she cried just above a whisper, "Do you believe it; you guys are on TV!" As my tired eyes slowly focused in on the television screen, I saw the three of us in action, sitting side by side in the stands at Busch Stadium in St. Louis eating peanuts and Cracker Jack. There were at least twenty five people in the room; three were reading and twenty-two had their eyes glued to the television, yet not a soul recognized me, attesting to the fact that together we were a noteworthy item; individually we were nothing.

The Three Extras

Two hours had passed before Willy ventured out from the examining area and into the waiting room. Joanna and I jumped to our feet and rushed over to greet him. "Is she okay?" Joanna asked worriedly.

"She's going to be fine," Willy said with a sigh of relief, "She has, of all things, diverticulitis! They medicated her and she's feeling much better!"

"Diverticulitis," I questioned, "How the fuck did she get that?"

"Who the heck knows, but thank God that's all it was!"

Tracy was released from the hospital with strict dietary instructions and a stack of prescriptions, a sad sign of our inescapable aging. We followed Willy back home and put our previous plans of eating and drinking on hold.

Two weeks after Tracy's gastric episode came the long-awaited call from Wendy. She had been swamped with offers from dozens of noteworthy directors, studios and advertising agencies and requested we come to New York as soon as possible to discuss scheduling. Jack contacted Willy immediately after hearing from Wendy and asked if it would be alright if Jenny came to Florida to hang with Joanna and Tracy while the three of us were away. The news of Tracy's mishap had Jenny feeling as if she needed to spend some time with her enduring friends. As long as we were going to be away, it gave Willy some peace of mind to know his wife wouldn't be left alone. Since his daughters were busy with families of their own, Willy didn't want to burden them with having to keep an eye on their mother.

Jack and Jenny arrived on a Friday night. The six of us spent a quiet weekend pampering Tracy and seeing to it that she stuck to her diet and took her medication. On Monday morning,

Jack, Willy and I were once again waving goodbye to the girls as the limo pulled out of our driveway to carry us off to yet another airport. As we crawled along Interstate 95 in stop and go traffic, Willy wondered out loud, "How much longer do you think we're gonna be able to do this, guys?"

"We just got started," Jack answered in his familiar take-charge manner, "We just got started!"

It had been a while since we had seen Wendy. Nothing changed; she was still a bubbly ball of energy. Her office still looked as though she had left the windows open during a hurricane. Papers, magazines and show business periodicals were strewn about all over. She had greeted each of us with a warm but quick embrace because she was anxious to get down to business. "Boys, I'm simply overwhelmed by all the options we have! It seems that everybody in show biz has an interest in the Three Extras!" Clearing away a stack of papers from her well-worn leather couch, she motioned for us to take a seat.

"So Wendy," I inquired enthusiastically, "It sounds as if we're going to be busy for a while; what do you got?"

"Fellows, this is even mind-boggling to me. I've been in this business a very long time and have never experienced the demands for screen personalities like the ones I've been getting for you! To be quite honest, sometimes I get the feeling someone's playing a practical joke on me and my agency!"

"Gee thanks!" Willy chuckled, "Some vote of confidence!"

"No, no, that's not what I mean," Wendy corrected herself, "I love you guys. I fell in love with your look and your charisma from the day I first set eyes on you. It's just that there are millions of inspiring actors and actresses out there who would kill to be in your position, but for some crazy reason, you three are the hot topic!"

"Hey! When you got it, you got it!" Jack boasted.

Wendy shuffled paper after paper rattling off proposals as if she'd just graduated from an Evelyn Wood speed reading course.

"Whoa! Slow down," Jack interrupted, "How in the world do you expect us to accomplish all that in the few years we have left in our lives?"

"That's precisely why it was imperative we have this meeting. There are some major decisions to be made and they have to be made quickly! The folks at the agency who produced the Master Card ads have been approached by Anheuser-Busch to perform the same marketing magic and naturally they inquired about your availability. A major pharmaceutical company wants to use you three in an ongoing ad for a new pill on the market for erectile dysfunction. On top of that, execs at ABC came up with a concept for a series about three retired guys who become movie extras and they want to discuss the possibility of creating a series based upon your experiences!"

"So what's the problem?" Willy asked.

"The problem is that almost every director in Hollywood is looking to have the three of you appear in their upcoming movies. I know this is going to sound like some kind of a joke, but since attendance at movies has been on a rapid decline, somebody in tinsel town came up with the brainstorm of making you guys the 'Where's Waldo' of the film world!"

"Just what the hell are you proposing," Jack demanded, "It sounds preposterous!"

"That's exactly what I thought at first, but if the studios are willing to pay big bucks for your three mugs, I say we go with it! Strike while the iron's hot!"

"I'm still not sure I understand where this is going," I asked curiously but skeptically.

"Listen, whether you know it or not, everything in this world is contrived. The powers that be can make the masses buy into almost anything. You three just happened to be in the right place at the right time."

"Go on," I said, twirling my fingers above my head motioning for her to continue, "Sell me!"

"Sometime in the next week or so, you guys are going to be getting an invitation to the world premier of the film *River Rats* and there is strong talk circulating among Hollywood heavies that the Academy will be creating a new category for best performance by an extra. You didn't hear it from me, but you three are going to win and once you do, The Three Extras are going to be a huge box office draw!"

"That's crazy!" Jack muttered as he rose from the couch and paced the room like an expectant father, "You're tainting my perception of the movie business. It's almost like a congressman admitting he sold his vote or the government disclosing that 9-11 was an inside job!"

"Exactly, but don't unearth feelings I've tried so hard to bury by changing the subject, my friend. We've got lots to discuss. It's no time for a conversation on past politics and conspiracy theories!"

"Sorry," Jack replied, "Well over a decade later and it's still a sore subject. Get back to 'Where's Waldo!'"

"Okay," Wendy continued, "With your consent, which I've been strongly advised to make you give me, you'll be popping up in at least two dozen major productions in the upcoming year. The plan is to persuade directors to include the three of you in quick, almost subliminal-like, random scenes, and to challenge movie audiences to correctly identify where and

The Three Extras

when each of you appears in the film. If the gimmick succeeds, who can tell how long they will milk it!"

"My God," I uttered in disbelief, "This sounds too weird. It's almost as if they're making a mockery of their own profession!"

"When push comes to shove, Johnny boy, it all comes down to money! And if having The Three Extras appear in every other movie is going to boost ticket sales, then why should it matter! As Woody Allen once put it, take the money and run! And we're talking a fair amount of money here gentlemen!"

Unusually indecisive, Jack paced about in random circles not sure of exactly what to say, but managed to ask a question anyway, "But what about ABC and the idea they have for a series; isn't television the way to go?"

"Too risky," Wendy replied assertively, "No guarantees concerning how long it will take before the pilot is written and there's always the chance of the big wigs losing interest. The studios, on the other hand, are anxious and ready to enter into negotiations. Shooting schedules for most of the films have been arranged, it's just a matter of logistics and getting you to where you're needed!"

"Wendy, what about the commercials?" asked Willy, "Why wouldn't we just stick to what made us successful in the first place, commercials?"

"Have I steered you guys wrong yet? Commercials are iffy. There's no guarantee they get aired, and if they do, how long before they get pulled? We just happened to strike gold with Master Card. Trust me; the movies are a sure thing. One day I promise you, the name The Three Extras will be on theatre marquees all over the world!"

Jack stopped pacing. He turned to face Willy and me and as he's done for as long as we've known him, spoke on our behalf, "Well Wendy, it seems like you made our minds up for us. Where do we sign and where are we headed next?"

"Not so fast," I interjected, "Why can't we do both, commercials and films? After all, it's only a matter of time before these charming faces of ours lose their allure!"

Wendy smiled as dollar signs sparkled in her eyes, "I can give you as much as you're willing to handle and gamble!"

We had to remain in New York for two weeks to meet with agents, attorneys and various other show business personnel. Wendy instructed her staff to coordinate our schedules, arrange for our travelling and pretty much orchestrate our lives for the coming year. When Wendy revealed the names of the actors and actresses we'd be working with and the directors whose films we'd be appearing in, we were floored. When I saw Wendy's mouth form the words Tim Burton, Brad Pitt and Natalie Portman I had to laugh, thinking to myself, "This is crazy, who the hell are we?" Because Tracy's health was constantly on his mind, Willy wasn't overly excited about having to travel so much, but remembering the pact we made, it's the three of us or none of us, he agreed to go along with whatever it was Jack and I decided to do.

We made my house in Long Island home base whenever we were in New York. Willy and Tracy had already made the decision to make West Palm Beach their permanent address and put their New York residence up for sale. Even though Joanna was getting accustomed to the Florida climate, we still weren't comfortable with the idea of giving up our Wantagh residence. Wendy accommodated us by making certain we had breaks in our schedules, allowing us to spend a little time at home every few weeks. To be honest, the constant travelling was draining not only for ourselves, but for our families. Not only did we

The Three Extras

rarely get to see our wives, but trying to arrange our lives so we could get to see our kids and our grandkids was becoming extremely difficult. But we each knew our streak of good fortune wasn't going to last, so we pushed ourselves to do whatever was necessary to make as much money as possible to allow us to live the upscale lifestyle we were beginning to get used to.

After Jack's close call with Veronica Pond in Hawaii and after witnessing Tracy sprawled out on her kitchen floor writhing in pain, somehow show business suddenly became more job than merriment. I don't know if it was a temporary post mid-life crisis we each had to experience, but the partying and the glamour had suddenly lost its appeal. Our over-the-hill, thrill seeking mind-set had turned to one of out-and-out professionalism. Now it had become a matter of getting the job done, moving on to the next, adding to our bank accounts and getting home. I underwent a brief period not being able to forgive myself for the one night stand I had in Sedona and agonized over the possibility of Joanna ever finding out.

It was hard to believe we were in our mid-sixties and traveling around the globe like jet-setters. The following year found us everywhere from Alaska to Zaire and in the company of so many renowned directors and actors, and dozens of up and coming stars. It was ridiculously odd how we were getting VIP treatment, even more so than the stars like Sean Penn, Johnny Depp, Jude Law and Jonah Hill. We were looked upon as major players with very tight schedules and were dealt with as top priority. As soon as we arrived on a set, all attention was ours until the director was satisfied with the shots. We weren't afforded the time to remain in any one place for more than forty-eight hours because somewhere in the world another director was waiting to add our mugs to his or her contribution to the industry's "Find the Three Extras" project. Sometimes we appeared together, sometimes we appeared separately, but it was the filmmakers' assignment to somehow incorporate our scenes inconspicuously into a movie, not making it challenging for moviegoers to spot us.

We were cast as everything from merchants in a Middle Eastern trading village, to clerks in a Little Rock, Arkansas bowling alley, to Cardinals at the Vatican in Rome. One thing was for sure, we really did get to see the world, if only in brief glances. Of all the sets we were on, I think my favorite was when we were on location in Egypt for a film entitled, "Sky Men." The movie was based on a story of a group of blacklisted US scientists who follow their gut feelings and discover information in the Pyramids revealing the origins of human life. My only regret was that we couldn't have stayed longer. In all of our travels, the Pyramids had to be the most fascinating structures I'd ever seen.

As we bounced from country to country, city to city, Wendy made it a point to keep in continuous contact with us. She was still entertaining the idea of having us do the pharmaceutical ad for the new wonder drug called Stiphenal, a pill enabling men with erectile dysfunction to perform on the spot as if they were teenage boys. The commercial was to be shot on location in Las Vegas and alluded to the suggestion that three widowed old timers can still have the time of their lives with younger women. Because of the tremendous success of the Master Card ads, the production company insisted on casting the three of us in the commercial and was willing to pay a huge amount of money. Money talks, so Wendy accepted the deal on our behalf.

While we were hard at work in Vegas, walking arm in arm with bosomy, beautiful young ladies, in and out of hotel lobbies, restaurants and nightclubs, we received the call from Wendy announcing we had been officially nominated for an Academy Award as best extras. "She wasn't kidding," I said to my partners, "They're really going through with this whole thing. It's insane!"

"No crazier than David Spade being a movie star," Jack quickly replied, "Stranger things have happened!"

Immediately we called home with the good, yet preposterous news about our nominations. "Start shopping for a fancy dress," I warned Joanna, "you're going to Hollywood!"

By the time our big night arrived, we had begun work on another commercial and already appeared before the cameras in over twenty-three films with thirteen remaining to fulfill our commitment. We were definitely burning the candle at both ends, but at the same time, we were securing our financial future.

Swarms of paparazzi and movie fans lined the sunny streets surrounding the Apple Theatre. Jack, Willy and I, along with our wives, arrived by limousine and were escorted past the crowds and into the theater where we posed for a series of photos and brief interviews. Reporters were shoving microphones in front of our faces and asking questions, such as, how we felt going from relative obscurity to being nominated for an Oscar. "It's all about being in the right place at the right time," Jack replied humbly, "We were very lucky!" The girls looked stunning in their rented designer gowns, and all eyes were on the six of us, the talk of Hollywood, as the ushers led us to our seats.

Not only was *River Rats* nominated for Best Picture and the three of us for Best Performance by an Extra, but Veronica Pond was up for Best Supporting Actress. Jack was well aware of the possibility that Jenny and Veronica could meet that evening and he was going to do anything and everything in his power not to let that happen. Jenny still had no name or face to connect to the Hawaii incident and Jack wanted to keep it that way!

The Oscar celebration was everything we thought it might be, a sea of superficial glamour with herds of folks just craving to be seen: actors, actresses, directors, producers and behind the scenes people, all addicted to the attention, approval and admiration of others. It was really pretty nauseating.

The entire evening was highly orchestrated and very contrived. Many winners were notified beforehand and told to limit their acceptance speeches to a given time frame. As much as it appears to be a spontaneous event when we watch from our living rooms, it is far from it. There was tremendous pressure coming from network executives to keep the festivities moving along, the commercials aired and the whole thing wrapped up by late night news time! Every word was scripted and there was no room for improvising.

An usher approached our row, motioned for our attention and told us that we had five minutes until we would be summoned to the stage. It felt very weird knowing we were in cahoots on a scheme created solely to boost box office sales. With motion pictures so readily available and easily accessible for home viewing, movie theaters were in danger of soon becoming extinct. It was their hope The Three Extras could save the day. The announcer's booming, persuasive voice got the crowd's attention when he called out the presenters names for the next award; "Ladies and gentlemen, presenting the award for Best Extras, last year's Best Supporting Actress for her role in *Tenders* and this year's nominee for Best Supporting Actress for *River Rats*, Marisa Tomei and Veronica Pond!"

The Three Extras

"Oh my fucking Lord," Willy moaned, "Of all the people in Hollywood!"

When the applause died down, Marisa Tomei stepped up to the microphone, glanced over the room, giggled and then read from the cue cards: "Ladies and gentlemen, colleagues...I am honored to be presenting for the very first time in Oscar's history, an award category that has long been overdue, The Extra. The faces that have continued to go unnoticed, yet at the same time have brought a sense of realism to motion pictures, are finally getting the recognition they so deserve! The movie extras work hard at achieving the expressions and the movements sought by directors in making their films appear true to life. The movie extras supply the background and support needed for actors and actresses to perform to their best ability. I had the privilege of working with tonight's winners and can say from experience these fellows are three of the nicest guys you'll ever meet aside from being so easy and pleasant to work with...and they're kind of cute to boot!"

"Oh Jesus," Jenny groaned, "kind of cute!"

Marisa smiled and stepped back as Veronica tore open the envelope before approaching the microphone. "Ladies and gentlemen, members of the Academy, it is our pleasure to present the Oscar for Best Extra to three of the hardest working guys in Hollywood...Jack, Willy and John, or as we affectionately know them, The Three Extras!"

The usher beckoned us to rise from our seats and move quickly towards the stage. The crowd went wild with applause as we neared the podium while the scenes from *River Rats* featuring us appeared on the huge screen in the background. To me, it was quite obvious that Veronica still hungered for Jack. As he took the Oscar from her hands, her eyes were fixed upon him and glowed with desire. She kissed him on the cheek as she congratulated him. At the same time, I observed Marisa sneakily give Willy a pinch on his thigh. It was evident to me that both my partners were suddenly flustered, so I had almost no choice but to override the plan and make our acceptance speech in place of Jack. "On behalf of Willy and Jack, I would like to thank the Academy for recognizing the role of the movie extra and bestowing this prestigious award upon us. We would also like to thank our wives for their patience and understanding and allowing us at this time in our lives to experience the travels and thrills of the movie business...Thank you!" Before I could get out my last syllable, the orchestra kicked in, and before we knew it, the three of us, along with Veronica and Marisa, were escorted off the stage by two of the most ravishing young models we'd ever seen. Backstage personnel pointed the way along the corridors leading to the auditorium, and as soon as she was certain we were off camera, Veronica drew nearer to Jack.

"So nice to finally see you again, Jack! Congratulations! How exciting this must be for you!"

"Nice to see you too, Veronica...Yeah, it is kind of exciting," a jittery Jack answered, hoping there was no way Jenny would ever make the connection, "and I see you're up for an award yourself this evening!"

"Oh, I know, it really is thrilling! Say, maybe we can hook up and celebrate at the after- party later tonight!"

Jack reached for his handkerchief, wiped his brow and lied, "Uh, sure thing Veronica, I'll look for you..."

Meanwhile, Marisa had cornered Willy, threw her arms around him, gave him a quick kiss on the lips, and like an enthusiastic cheer leader, happily shrieked, "I'm so excited for you guys! This is wonderful!"

"Geez, girls," Willy whined while constantly looking over his shoulder, "Our wives are in the audience!"

"Oh Willy," Marisa giggled, "We're just happy for you! No harm in that now, is there sweetie?"

As we walked past the entrance doors to the theater, the girls went their separate ways waving with the kind of body language that forewarned my colleagues if they cared to remain out of trouble, avoid them at all costs. Ushers led us back to our seats where we rejoined our wives.

"Congratulations guys," Tracy's bubbling voice cried out, "You looked so cool up there! Veronica Pond is so beautiful!"

"She's alright," Jack said snappishly.

"You don't think she's gorgeous?" Jenny asked.

"I said she's okay," Jack repeated, "I think those two models are way more beautiful!"

"Yeah," Jenny continued, "but they're also about ten years younger!"

"Who cares," Willy nervously interjected, "Just drop it…everybody's gorgeous at these things!"

"Wow, aren't you a little high strung, Willy Taylor! What's eating you?"

"Nothing," Willy huffed, "I just can't wait for this to be over!"

As usual, the pomp and circumstance of Oscar night seemed to go on forever. Jenny, Joanna and Tracy were enjoying themselves as they stargazed, trying to inconspicuously point out who they recognized. Jack and Willy were getting antsy with apprehension over an inevitable encounter between Marisa, Veronica and their wives. I slouched down into my seat taking in all the energy in the room and tried my best to make sense of things. The fact that we were actually present at the Academy Awards seemed totally ridiculous in itself. Certainly I was enjoying the benefit of reaping the rewards, but I felt, undeservedly so. I felt as if some higher power randomly singled us out and decided to turn our ordinary lives into a story book fantasy. It also seemed completely absurd, a little bizarre, in fact, to see my two best friends, now in their sixties, acting like clumsy, guilt-ridden high school boys, trying to protect their lifelong marriages by avoiding the relatively harmless advances of two extremely successful, talented, outgoing actresses.

When the evening's festivities came to a close, the crowd rose to their feet and made their way out to the street where cameras flashed, limousines waited and news reporters hustled to get interviews. We stopped to pose at least a dozen times and answered an unrelenting barrage of questions from entertainment journalists before reaching our ride.

"How does it feel to be the first recipients of this award?" asked a reporter hungry for a new angle on an old story.

"Surreal!" I remarked as we climbed into the back of our limo.

"What does the future hold for The Three Extras?" the determined reporter pressed while stretching his microphone towards us for our reply.

"Hopefully, steady work and fat bank accounts," Jack answered as the door shut and we pulled away into the congested Hollywood streets.

Jack and Willy were noticeably relieved that we had made it out of the theater without encountering Marisa and Veronica. We were very much aware that our winning an Oscar was deliberately calculated, and, for the most part, our immediate futures were set in stone. We agreed to pass on the many invitations we received to attend Oscar after-parties at the local clubs and restaurants and unanimously agreed to spend the remainder of the evening in the company of our wives at a low-profile, quaint, after hours place out of the Hollywood area. It was only a matter of time before we were recognized by a few of the patrons who were sitting at the bar nursing their drinks while watching the news.

"Hey, congratulations! You're those three extra guys," a stout man resembling Danny De Vito called out, turning his attention away from his baked clams.

"You must be mistaken," Jack laughed, "never heard of them!"

"Pretty funny," the fellow replied, and then made his way over to our table with a napkin and a pen. "Can I get your autographs?"

"Not unless you give us yours," Jack quipped to a blank stare.

After we signed his napkin, with a handshake and a wink, Jack diplomatically told him we were trying to have a quiet evening with our wives. "I get it," the man complied with a Mafioso attitude and Brooklyn accent, "I'll see to it nobody bothers you!"

Our exhilarating evening was followed by a restful stay at a posh LA hotel where each of us spent the remaining hours getting reacquainted with our spouses. The morning after, Jenny headed back to San Diego while Joanna and Tracy made their way back home to Florida. Jack, Willy and I had to return to Vegas for a few more days to complete the Stiphenal commercial.

John Rullo

~WHEN YOU LEAST EXPECT IT~

The year that followed was no doubt the busiest of our lives. We fulfilled our commitment by completing scenes in over thirty-six movies. The Stiphenal commercials became one of the most successful ad campaigns in television history, and articles featuring The Three Extras were appearing in newspapers and magazines worldwide. It was also the year when the Motion Picture Industry introduced the "Find the Three Extras" contest. "Three Extras" merchandise was being sold in theaters, gift shops, department stores: anything from tee-shirts and refrigerator magnets to key chains and bumper stickers. It was absolutely mind-boggling to witness how a phenomenon could be created and how the masses could be so easily manipulated. Our name was popping up everywhere. To see the words "Featuring the Three Extras" up in lights on the marquees of the neighborhood theaters right alongside the biggest names in Hollywood was truly a kick for each of us, but needless to say, baffling as well.

Financially, we were better off than we had ever imagined possible. We were living extremely comfortable lives while the majority of the country was existing on austerity budgets, barely managing to squeak by. Our children's and grandchildren's futures were secure. Our dreams had come true, more or less, and it all happened quite unexpectedly. None of us had ever conceived that at this stage of our lives, our late sixties, such good fortune would have fallen into our laps. As it is with almost everything in life, however, things started to get old rather quickly for Willy and me. The traveling was getting wearisome and we agreed we needed to take a well-deserved break. Jack, on the other hand, felt we still had a few good years in us and wanted to work as long as the offers kept coming in. Wendy had become somewhat of a slave driver, trying to persuade us to take on as much work as humanly possible. Her philosophy was similar to Jack's, that is, strike while the iron is hot; take it when you can get it. As much as we understood their business sense, Willy and I stood our ground and refused to take on any more work for at least six months. Life seemed to be on fast-forward; seventy was right around the corner, and we were feeling the need to enjoy our families and our new homes while we were still able to.

    I don't know if it was partially due to the luxuries our financial wellbeing allowed us to have, but Joanna and I were getting along better than ever. She and I and Willy and Tracy became inseparable again, hanging at each other's houses, going out to dinner, spending days at the beach and enjoying extended visits from our kids and our grandchildren. Not a day went by without a call from Jack, however, who kept nudging us about getting back to work. Wendy knew Willy and I stood firm on lying low for a while, so she stopped calling. Instead, she continued to contact Jack with tantalizing offers and hopes that maybe he could convince us to cut our extended vacation short.

    "Come on guys," Jack would beseech, "How much longer are we going to be able to do this?"

    "Johnny and I need to chill for a few months," Willy explained, "We'll get back on board soon, I promise!"

    As much as we were enjoying our much needed time of rest and relaxation, we were feeling a bit guilty about not cooperating with Jack; after all, if it weren't for his initial vision and drive, we'd still be living on fixed incomes in Long Island.

It was only because we were feeling at fault that we eventually broke down and agreed to meet Jack in New York for an appearance on Jimmy Fallon. The producers of the late-night show had been unrelenting in their requests for The Three Extras interview. We had never appeared on a talk show before, and since Fallon's ratings had dropped considerably when veteran comedian Dennis Blair took over Letterman's spot, they had high hopes that we could produce the same positive results for the show that we did for movie theater box offices.

It was in June of 2020 when Willy and I finally met up with Jack in New York. Seeing how eager and happy he was to be reunited with us dissolved any remaining reluctance we initially had about leaving Florida. After a successful appearance on Fallon's show, the three of us had dinner with Wendy at Renaldo's, Jack's favorite Manhattan Italian restaurant. Renaldo's was a quaint little place on 10th Avenue and 56th Street, where Jack had been dining since his days working for Macy's. Hanging on the wall behind the bar was an 8 X 10 black and white autographed photo of the three of us with Martin Scorsese and Marisa Tomei. Jack had given it to Renaldo the very first time The Three Extras had dined there together, and ever since then, we've been given the red carpet treatment whenever we were in town. Wendy was beginning to show her age and we often wondered if and when she ever planned on retiring. Nevertheless, she was still the little fireball of energy she'd always been and couldn't wait to discuss future projects, one of which was the ABC series based upon our very own success story. Our waiter brought over a bottle of Jack's favorite Chianti, and before he even got the cork out, my cell device alerted me that Joanna was calling.

"Hey, Babe, what's up?" I asked.

I could tell by the tremble in her voice something was terribly wrong. "John, you better get Willy home as soon as humanly possible; an ambulance is on the way to bring Tracy to the ER. She's doubled over in pain!"

"Okay, Joanna," I said trying to remain calm, "I'll break it to him and try to get us on a flight ASAP!"

Jack immediately sensed there was a problem and inquired, "Everything okay, Johnny?"

"Listen, I hate to break up this little gathering," I said calmly, "but Willy and I need to get back home…"

"What's going on John?" Willy said uneasily while dropping his breadstick onto his plate.

"Tracy's on her way to the hospital and Joanna's with her…"

Before I could complete my thought Willy cut in, "What did she say happened…?"

"She doubled over in pain just like she did the last time…"

Willy jumped up from his chair, looked at me frantically and said, "We got to go!"

Trying my best to keep him calm, I said, "Relax. Everything is going to be fine."

Wendy immediately began to investigate travel possibilities on her phone and found available seats on a flight leaving JFK in a few hours. Jack apologized to Renaldo, explaining the urgent situation to which he was totally sympathetic. We regretted cutting our dinner short with Wendy, but she certainly understood. "Everything is going to be fine," Wendy said in an earnest effort to offer Willy some moral support, and didn't leave us until we were in a cab and on our way to the airport. Instead of returning home to California, Jack decided to remain with us and come to Florida.

Willy was silent for most of the trip. His complexion had turned sickly pale and his watery eyes revealed that he was thinking the worst.

"I knew we shouldn't have taken this trip," he moaned, "We should have stood our ground and stayed home."

"Should've, could've, would've," I answered consolingly, "You had no idea this would happen…Don't blame yourself. Everything's going to be alright."

We arrived at Good Samaritan Hospital at 9:45 that evening. Joanna was in the lobby. She greeted us with emotional hugs and apparent uneasiness.

"Is she alright?" Willy asked Joanna as his hands shook uncontrollably and his head turned from side to side.

"Willy," Joanna answered gently, "They had to perform emergency surgery. Tracy's appendix burst…"

"How the fuck," Willy cried out, once again blaming himself for not being with her when it happened, "I should have never gone to New York…"

"I called your kids to let them know what's going on and they'll be here tomorrow."

Willy didn't know which way to turn or what to do. He gave Joanna the tightest embrace and then went to the front desk where he announced his arrival and demanded to see Tracy's doctor as soon as possible. There was nothing the four of us could do except to pace the floors of the hospital lobby and wait.

The next couple of hours felt like an eternity. Our eyes were glued to the clock on the wall and we jerked to attention every time a doctor in scrubs happened to pass through the lobby. Each of us took turns pacing the floor with Willy, trying our best to console him, but for some odd reason he kept repeating how he had a premonition the news we were about to hear wasn't going to be good. He couldn't hold back his tears and Joanna kept feeding him tissues from her purse.

"I don't know what I would do without her," he sobbed.

"What are you talking about?" Joanna reprimanded, "She's in good care; she's going to be fine!"

Just then, we noticed a doctor fully draped in blue scrubs and matching surgical mask come up to the front desk and direct a question to the receptionist. As he pointed towards us, she nodded, and with head facing downward, he slowly approached Willy and asked, "Mr. Taylor?"

At this time in our lives, almost everyone appeared to be younger than we were, especially doctors and policemen. The doctor couldn't have been much older than thirty. He had a very mild demeanor and the solemn look in his deep blue eyes tipped us off that what he was about to say wasn't going to be pleasant. Holding a computer clip board in his left hand, he extended his right arm and shook hands with Willy.

"Hello, doctor, I'm Willy Taylor; how is Tracy?"

"Hi, Mr. Taylor, I'm Doctor Janssen…I wish I had better news for you," he said softly as Jack, Jenny, Joanna and I stood behind Willy listening carefully. Jack and I placed our hands firmly upon Willy's shoulders as the youthful doctor continued. "Your wife must have been suffering with appendicitis for quite some time. How she had been withstanding the discomfort is anybody's guess. Her appendix burst, which required immediate emergency surgery, but to complicate matters, the infection spread unusually fast, causing her to go into septic shock…."

As Doctor Janssen spoke, his discouraging words seemingly put Willy in a trance. In an involuntary effort to guard his heart, he tried to block out any further distressing news. He could scarcely comprehend anything the doctor was trying to explain to him and as his knees weakened and buckled under him, he motioned that he needed to sit. Willy sat with his head in his hands as the sympathetic doctor gently repeated the complications of Tracy's surgery and the seriousness of her sudden illness.

"Can I please see her," Willy begged.

"Maybe just for a few minutes, Mr. Taylor, she's in recovery. The best thing you can do at the moment is to go home and get some rest and I'll see you back here in the morning."

All of us were deeply upset and trying our utmost to keep Willy encouraged by masking our own worry and suppressing our fears. In all the years I'd known Willy, I have never seen him so distraught and confused. He wasn't able to verbalize his thoughts and he wandered the lobby like a lost puppy. While Joanna and Jack took hold of him and unsuccessfully tried to lead him out of the hospital to our car, I stood back to further question the doctor.

"I'm so sorry," he said in a heartfelt sigh, "What happened to Mrs. Taylor is very uncommon. I have never seen infection spread so quickly. The toxins in her body have caused multisystem organ failure. She is being heavily medicated in our best attempt to fight off the infection and hopefully allow her lungs and kidneys to function normally. Please relay to Mr. Taylor that we will do everything in our power to make her come out of this. By the way, I hope I'm not being out of line, but I loved you guys in *River Rats*."

I didn't know what to say and I especially didn't know how to break the news to Willy. I couldn't believe what was happening and the thought of losing Tracy was devastating. I joined the others in trying to convince Willy it would be best to follow the doctor's orders by heading home, even though I was fairly certain we were all bound to have a sleepless night. Willy refused to leave, and since I didn't think it was a good idea for him to spend the night alone, I stayed behind while Joanna and Jack went back to our place and hammered down shots of Jack Daniels until sunrise. Willy and I managed to doze off periodically during a night we thought would never end. Looking like lost souls, Joanna and Jack returned to the hospital at the crack of dawn with coffee and some blueberry muffins Joanna had whipped up at home.

Tracy was in ICU and only for brief moments was Willy permitted to look in on her as a medical team ineffectively strived to keep her stable. Somehow he found the strength to stand beside her as she silently struggled to remain alive with the help of the life support system. She didn't respond to any of the treatments, and her condition worsened through the night. A nurse accompanied Willy back to the lobby where we waited, and he, looking as if he were just hit by a truck, went to pieces. Dr. Janssen reassured us they were doing everything medically possible to see to it that Tracy survived and promised to keep us continually updated of any progress. Jack had just called Jenny to tell her the news when Hannah and Rachel, Willy and Tracy's daughters, entered the lobby. Neither of them was aware of the extent of their mom's illness, but one look at their dad, and the gloom showing in our faces, clued them in that circumstances were not good. They held their father tightly and asked when they could see their mom. Time dragged, the minutes feeling like hours, as we patiently waited, walking in circles about the hospital lobby, drinking coffee from paper cups, praying and wondering.

"I think you and your immediate family should spend a few moments with your wife," Dr. Janssen compassionately suggested, "She's struggling…"

Willy aged twenty years in those few seconds. Hannah and Rachel burst into tears as they tightly gripped Willy's arms.

Bracing their dad to keep him on his feet, the three of them followed the doctor through the corridors leading to the room where Tracy clung to life. Jack, Joanna and I remained in the lobby huddled together on a couch, hoping the sick emptiness we were feeling was all part of a bad dream, the equalizer to the fairy tale we were living. Not even an hour later, Willy and his daughters returned to the lobby, choking on the tears they were ineffectively trying to hold back. Joanna squeezed my hand so tightly I could feel my knuckles crack as Jack quavered, "Oh my God, no!" We dashed across the worn and faded floor of the lobby into a long supportive group hug with Willy and the girls. Willy's tears began to gush out uncontrollably while he moaned the most sorrowful words I have ever heard, "Tracy's dead…"

Tracy had made her wishes known long before she died. She always said if she was the first of us to go, she didn't want a wake or a big funeral. Her desire was to be cremated and for Willy to take her ashes with him wherever he goes. Willy would later honor her wishes even to the point where he had some of her ashes placed inside a gold plated capsule that he wore on a chain in place of the crucifix that had always dangled from his neck. Jenny flew in from California the day after Tracy passed. When her eyes met Willy's, the flow of tears was unstoppable. For a while, none of us were capable of even facing one another without uncontrollable sobbing. In an effort to respect what Tracy wanted, only our immediate families were informed and within twenty-four hours, all of our kids had arrived. With the three of us having been on the road so often, it was a very long time since we've all been able to gather as a group. The last time my kids saw Tracy and Willy's girls was at their weddings. Wherever Tracy's spirit was dwelling, I knew she was smiling at the thought of us all being together. After a short memorial service at the crematorium, we all had dinner at Mario's of West Palm, once Tracy's restaurant of choice. We had the back room all to ourselves, and the staff couldn't have been more accommodating. Having our kids among us was a pleasant but bittersweet distraction. The conversations centered on all the happy times and wonderful memories. It was one of those afternoons we never wanted to end, but as it is with all things, time quickly passed. Before we knew it, a week had gone by, and life drew everybody back into its rat race.

Rachel and Hannah wanted Willy to return to New York with them, but he preferred to stay put in Florida. Joanna and I assured them we would never let him out of our sight, and for the next month or so we were together morning, noon and night. Some evenings, Willy would just nod out on our living room couch after a few Jack and gingers, and remain there until we woke him for breakfast the following morning. Jack was getting antsy and suggested that perhaps getting back in front of a camera would do Willy some good. Every few days he would call from the west coast to ask if I thought our partner was ready to get back to work. The truth was I didn't know how to answer because I never wanted to bring it up. Wendy was pushing for the ABC special while The Three Extras craze was still newsworthy. From what I could tell, however, working was the furthest thing from Willy's mind. I promised Jack I would gently bring up the subject when I thought the timing was appropriate.

John Rullo

~DIDN'T WE JUST DO THIS? ~

It had been eight months since Tracy's death when Willy just happened to mention Wendy and the ABC special. "Hey John," he nonchalantly asked, "Has anybody heard from Wendy? Has that idea for a show about us been shelved?"

It was good to see Willy coming out of his dark funk and giving thought to our careers again. I immediately contacted Jack to let him know Willy was showing signs of wanting to get on with his life. Jack, in turn, informed Wendy and requested a re-scheduling with ABC. In the meantime, Joanna started complaining of severe migraine headaches. I kept insisting she see a doctor but she assured me that the pains were nothing to get overly concerned about and continued to self-medicate with various painkillers and over the counter headache remedies. "I'm not very fond of Florida doctors," she would say ignoring my advice, "I'll see Dr. Genesee when we make a trip back to New York."

"By that time it may be too late," I would warn her with great exasperation to no avail, "I don't want there to be another widower among us!"

"I'm fine," she would persist, "They're just migraines."

It seemed like show time again. It was early on a Monday morning when Willy came over to our place with his carry-on. This time we were headed for Los Angeles, where ABC executives and writers were still excited about creating a series based on our story. We had another thirty minutes before the car service was expected to arrive so I told Willy to help himself to a cup of coffee.

"How's Joanna feeling today?" he asked in his familiarly caring way.

"Don't know yet. She's still in bed. She had a rough time falling asleep last night; the headaches started in again." I placed my breakfast dishes into the dishwasher and, while wiping off the kitchen counter, tried to convince myself she'd be fine while I was away. "I told her I was going to cancel this trip and take her to see a neurologist but she gets annoyed with me whenever I bring it up and keeps swearing she is fine. She popped a few pills and eventually fell asleep. I didn't want to wake her so I'll let her sleep until the car gets here."

"That's too bad," Willy said empathetically, "Are you sure you should be leaving her?"

"I called Daniel a few days ago; he's on the way down. He caught a flight out of MacArthur this morning and should be here by noon. He's going to spend the week with his mom!"

"That's good," Willy said, reassured, "I didn't want to say anything, but she probably shouldn't be left alone…"

Just then we heard the beeping of a car horn coming from my driveway. Willy gulped down the last drop of his coffee as I trotted upstairs to tell Joanna I was leaving. As I stepped into our bedroom and saw Joanna lying unusually still, stretched out on our bed face down, a sudden wave of nausea came over me. Something in my gut was sending me strong signals that all was not well. I walked over to the bed and whispered, "Joanna…Joanna, honey are you alright?" There was no response. Suddenly I felt something inside my chest snap as my heart dropped into the pit of my churning stomach to burn. I felt like I was going to vomit and crap simultaneously. I placed my arms around Joanna's motionless body and turned her over on her back. All I could see was the whites of her eyes and I cried, "Joanna, wake up, please wake up!" Deep down, I knew her spirit had fled from her body but I didn't want to believe it. I kissed her lips, I slapped her face. There was no sign of life, she wasn't breathing. Frenzied, I placed myself above her and tried desperately to breathe life into her. "Willy!" I screamed over and over so loudly I felt the muscles in my throat rip. I was frantic and irrational, hopelessly trying to shake her into consciousness when Willy came dashing into the room.

"Oh my God!" he shrieked and immediately reached for the phone to dial for help. Willy pried me off Joanna, pulled me from the bed and held me in his arms as tightly as he could, suddenly reliving the tragedy he went through less than a year before. I lost all composure and shook uncontrollably. I was unable to catch my breath, choked on the phlegm dripping down my throat and cried like a helpless, frightened, abandoned baby until I squeezed out every last tear.

I had a difficult time forgiving myself for not being more forceful with Joanna about seeing a doctor. As it turned out, the headaches were warning signs of the brain aneurysm that took her life. Daniel had arrived at the house just a few hours after the ambulance carried his mom away. When he saw I was still at home, he sensed something might be wrong and when I gently broke the news, he fell apart even worse than I did. One of the most difficult things I ever had to do, except for witnessing my son come totally apart before my eyes, was notifying my other two children about their mom passing away. The tears, the gasping and the silence over the phone were physical and mental torment; it felt as though someone was hammering red hot spikes into my already shattered heart. Willy was able to contact Jack and tell him the awful news before he had set out for L.A.

The Three Extras

He and Jenny were terribly shaken and made arrangements to get to Florida immediately. Jack assured Willy he would tend to business matters by having Wendy see to it our meeting was postponed indefinitely. At that moment, I could not care less about Wendy, ABC, the meeting, commercials or anything else that had to do with the Three Extras. I hated myself.

    I wasn't a religious man, and Joanna and I never discussed things like funerals, cemeteries and other unpleasantries. I had no idea if she preferred cremation over burial so I just assumed duplicating the identical proceedings Willy had done for Tracy made the most sense. It was a very painful time, but thank goodness, everything went smoothly. Having my two best friends on hand around the clock made the tragic event a little bit easier for me and the kids to withstand, but needless to say, life goes on, and when it was time for everyone to return to the daily routines, Natalie suggested I go back to New York to live with her family for a while. Just like Willy, I promised my beautiful daughter I would be alright remaining in Florida where Uncle Willy would be sure to look after me.

    It took about a month before I could sleep in my bed again. During that time, I spent some nights in the guest room, some nights curled up on the couch and some nights at Willy's place, where we became very fond of bourbon. It was so strange how Willy and I shared the same unfortunate, devastating events at what was probably the best time in our lives. I was starting to feel more and more like the old man I prided myself on never becoming. I decided to adopt the beach bum look by not shaving or cutting my hair. After all, I lived on the ocean, and having the beach in my backyard was very comforting. Willy and I spent many a day traipsing the length of the shoreline, soaking in the red glows and the green flashes of the sunsets. Some days we walked for miles and never spoke a word. Sometimes we talked incessantly about Tracy and Joanna, recalling all the happy times we shared through the decades. Sometimes we passed the hours asking countless unanswerable questions as to the purpose of life, the hereafter and why the lives of our wives were cut short. As despondent and embittered as we felt, we were also grateful we had each other to get through it. Not a day went by without us hearing from our kids or Jack and Jenny. Their continual love and support made us realize it would probably be healthier if we stopped brooding and got on with our lives. Jack was itching to get in his last licks as a screen star and we certainly owed it to him to cooperate.

One evening after Willy and I shared a grandma pizza and a bottle of wine at his place, we got a sudden desire for Irish coffee and spent at least an hour experimenting with assorted recipes in search of the perfect blend of coffee, cream and whiskey. After several failed attempts, we decided to call California for Jack's secret because he prepared the best Irish coffee either of us had ever tasted.

"First you need to mix the brown sugar with the Jameson's," he happily instructed us, and then quickly and intentionally changed the subject, "Hey, did you and Johnny happen to see the Stiphenall commercial was aired last night?"

"Why didn't you let us know?" Willy asked while rolling his eyes up at me, "Sure we would have liked to have seen it, but it will be on again!"

"What are you guys up to, having a party over there?"

"No, just had a yearning for Irish coffee and nobody can make it better than you," Willy said winking as he observed the mess we made on the kitchen counter. "We may as well learn from the best," he continued, "By the way, in case you're interested, Johnny and I agree that maybe you should call Wendy and ask her if she's got anything for us!"

"That's fantastic news," Jack's voice bubbled with excitement, "We're back!"

John Rullo

~IT WAS NICE WHILE IT LASTED~

Throughout the course of the next couple of years, Wendy kept us busy with appearances on talk shows, game shows and cameos on three major situation comedies. We also signed on to shoot a series of commercials for Aristotle's Holistic Health Resorts for seniors. We had established such an exceptionally good reputation in the business, casts and crews enjoyed having us on board and nobody could believe for a minute we were in our seventies. As long as there were no mirrors present, for the most part we felt like the same kids who tripped in the park, played in the clubs, and made movies in college. Those generations before us were wrong; it did not necessarily suck getting old! Although working was great therapy for Willy and me, we were usually homesick and looked forward to our breaks in the action. Jack, on the other hand, loved working, loved travelling and never seemed to tire of it.

Willy and I had returned to Florida after being on the road for six weeks. We weren't expected to be back on the west coast for about a month, so we made arrangements with our kids to visit with us during the time we were home. I had invited Jack and Jenny along, but they were planning a trip to New York to visit with their own family. Home just wasn't the same without Joanna's presence. No longer was there the ever-present scent of candles or the sound of music drifting through the house. She had always made it a point to have fresh cut flowers at the center of the dining room table and a variety of healthy plants hanging in the den. I didn't have a green thumb and so many of the thriving plants she had nursed from cuttings were parched, drooping and begging to be watered. I was so looking forward to seeing my sons and daughter with the hopes they would help to liven the place up a bit. Natalie was very much like her mom and when she arrived she didn't disappoint me. Her magic touch and rejuvenating spirit had the plants and flowers springing back to life in no time.

"Dad," she said, just like the school teacher she was, "What's so hard about asking a neighbor to stop in and give them a little water from time to time when you're away?"

"Oh stop nagging me," I babbled, "Can't think of everything!"

"You need to get a cleaning woman, dad," Natalie suggested kindly as she scribbled a heart in the dust on the kitchen table, "Look at this!"

"I miss your mom," I said sadly as I took in a deep breath and then exhaled, momentarily feeling remorse over the Arizona tryst that still taunted my conscience from time to time.

Our four week stretch at home with our loved ones was a bittersweet celebration. We were one big happy family commemorating Joanna and Tracy and being extremely grateful each of us could be there for one another. Our homes felt like retreat centers where everyone gathered to get reacquainted and share stories about the two ladies we missed so much. Tracy had been an aunt to my kids, as was Joanna to hers. Conversations were carried on much like group therapy sessions where tears mixed with laughter, broken hearts healed, and closure allowed everyone to finally get on with their lives. I took Natalie's advice and hired a cleaning service, a move that really came in handy once everyone left. It was staggering to come to grips with how quickly time had passed. Being on the road so often and relocating to Florida, I didn't get to witness on a daily basis the growth of my grandchildren. Newborns, in what seemed like moments ago, had grown into walking, talking, thinking people with unique personalities. I regretted having to share in the special times of their lives only through pictures and video conferences instead of being a hands-on grandfather. I was beginning to think I should be spending more time visiting with my kids and was seriously considering dropping out of the Three Extras. I had had enough. I was confident that Willy was having similar feelings, but somehow we were going to have to communicate these feelings to Jack.

Sometimes it's funny how things played out in our lives. Willy and I had unanimously decided to make one last trip to Los Angeles, finish shooting the commercial we were committed to do, and then drop the bomb on Jack. The day before we planned on going, however, I received a most disturbing call from Jenny. I've known Jenny for most of my life and just the sound of her voice when she spoke my name clued me in that something was terribly amiss.

"Johnny," she said in a raspy whisper followed by the sound of sobbing.

"Jenny, what happened?" I asked tensely.

There was a slight pause as she tried to gain her composure. "Last night Jack had a heart attack and possibly a stroke. I didn't want to call you guys until I knew what was going on for sure."

"We'll get on the very next flight out there," I said firmly.

"No, not yet, wait until you hear from me," she insisted, "The kids are flying in today. It'll just be too confusing. I promise I'll keep you posted."

"Please do, Jenny, and let us know if there's anything we can do."

The news came as a tremendous shock to Willy and me. As far as we could tell, Jack was the picture of health. Except for the heart attack he had before he retired and the unusual episode in Hawaii, since the day we embarked on our movie extra career, I couldn't recall his ever being sick even once. He was the one who kept pushing for us to take on more work. He never tired of the travelling or the other demands of the business. He was the one responsible for remaining in close contact with Wendy. We owed everything we had to Jack's passion and bottomless energy. We were feeling unjustifiably guilty about our intentions to retire. Although we were aching to be with our partner, we honored Jenny's wishes and waited until we got her approval. Just like he's done before, Willy took care of business, contacted Wendy and regretfully informed her that the ride had reached an end.

Over the next few days following Jenny's upsetting call, Willy and I floundered about like two lost souls, waiting anxiously for an update on our friend's condition. It was on a Friday afternoon when Jenny finally called asking us to make the trip. "I wish I had better news to report," she sighed, confirming that Jack suffered both a heart attack and minor stroke. "I know you guys have both been through a lot, but I think you should come see your friend."

We were able to book seats on a flight to California on very short notice, and so Saturday morning found us fastening our seatbelts on yet another airplane. From the moment we boarded, I caught one of the flight attendants, an attractive brunette probably in her early forties, quickly ogle us every so often. On one her many treks up and down the aisle checking to see if everyone's seats were in the upright position, she stopped at our row.

"Excuse me," she politely and discreetly asked, "Aren't there supposed to be three of you?"

Sensible enough to know she couldn't have been attracted to two old men, I figured she must have recognized us. I looked up at her and answered, "Actually we're on the way to meet up with him…"

"I loved *River Rats*; I was so moved by your performances!" she remarked with a wide-eyed smile. She paused for a second before handing me her pen and a cocktail napkin and asked, "I hope it's not too bold of me to request your autographs?"

Willy sniggered, "I guess two out of three ain't bad, huh?" As he took the pen from her hand he asked, "What's your name sweetheart?"

"Cindy," she answered timidly, seeming as if she may have been a little embarrassed to be disturbing us, "I'm so sorry to be bothering you!"

"Bothering us?" I laughed, "It's not every day someone asks for our autograph! It's our pleasure, Cindy!"

Willy and I happily obliged her and signed the napkin, "To Cindy, Warmest Regards; Willy Taylor and John Colletti/Two of the Three Extras!"

"Thank you so much," she whispered, "So nice to meet you! Tell the third extra I think you guys are great!"

We didn't say much to each other for the remainder of the trip. I was trying my best to keep thoughts of an incapacitated Jack from entering my head. I tried unsuccessfully to sleep, do crossword puzzles and read in attempts to avoid thinking about the cold, oppressive reality of aging and dying. Joanna and Tracy were gone and relatively speaking, so too was

The Three Extras

Jack. Willy and I were tired of acting and traveling, but no way did we expect our careers to end this way. Willy shifted his seat into the reclining position, and although he appeared to have fallen asleep, I could easily tell by his twitching fingers and fluttering eyelids that his restless mind was working overtime.

Hospitals had sadly become way too familiar for me and Willy. Walking into UC San Diego Medical Center gave me a nervous sinking feeling in my stomach as I recalled our recent hospital experiences. Jenny had given Willy and me perfectly detailed instructions on which elevator to take and which corners to turn in order to reach Jack's room. Our footsteps were perfectly synchronized as we paced ourselves along the long bluish green corridors, not at all eager to see what was waiting for us in Room 428.

We stood quietly at the entrance to Jack's room and saw Jenny sitting at his bedside reading an entertainment magazine. Jack was sitting, propped up by a pillow, with his mattress at a slight incline. His left arm was attached by tubes to intravenous bags feeding fluid into his veins one drop at a time. An assortment of wires stretched from areas on Jack's chest and skull to monitoring equipment where lights blipped simultaneously with beeps that sounded like the steady rhythm of a metronome. He seemed to be staring at the ceiling, oblivious to anything or anyone around him until we entered the room.

Jenny leaped out of her seat, tossed the magazine to the floor and cried out, "John Colletti and Willy Taylor!" She hugged the two of us with all her strength as shedding bittersweet tears, she sniffled, "I'm so glad you're here!" We stood side by side at the foot of Jack's bed gazing in disbelief. As his helpless eyes lit up, tears welled up in mine.

"Johnny...Willy," he slurred from the right side of his mouth as if he'd just learned to speak.

"How you doing, Jack," Willy spoke slowly, loudly and carefully enunciating every word.

"He's not deaf, for crying out loud!" I said, slapping Willy on the shoulder.

Jack lips tensed as he struggled to smile and as he rolled his eyes he mustered up enough strength to mumble, "Just great!"

There was an energy present in the room telling me unmistakably that Jack was pleased that we were there. But for the first time since the three of us bonded in high school, Jack wasn't in control, and the frustration showed in his furrowed brow. Jenny painstakingly explained the prognosis to Willy and me, which included his doctor's affirmation that after some time in rehabilitation, Jack's speech would begin to improve and eventually return to normal.

Willy and I had reserved rooms at a hotel midway between the hospital and Jenny's home, news that upset her when she heard. "I won't have it!" she said unbendingly, "You're staying at our place! Cancel your reservations!"

"You've got your family staying with you, Jenny, you don't need us adding to the confusion," I reasoned.

"I'm going to kick you, John Colletti...don't you dare insult me! You guys are staying with me. The boys are headed back to New York tonight and Lorraine is leaving Monday morning...Please, for me...I insist!"

"Alright," I conceded, "You twisted my arm!"

Our intentions were to stay only a week, but since our company seemed to be helping Jenny cope with the situation, we extended our stay. We did whatever we could to lighten her burden, decided to play it by ear and stay as long as necessary.

The Three Extras

Jack was released from the hospital on the Thursday after we arrived and transferred to a rehabilitation center located much closer to their home. Having us on board to share visits alleviated Jenny's load considerably. Jack had always taken care of her and suddenly roles were reversed. The visits were difficult only because Jack had such a hard time communicating. Sometimes we felt as if our presence was bothersome and we felt uneasy about pressuring him to speak. After a while, there wasn't much left to say. How often could we ask him how he was doing when we knew damn well he was miserable? Jack always enjoyed knowing what was going on in the entertainment world, so we would read him articles from the latest show business magazines. He would show signs of his approval or disapproval with grunts, nods or smiles. Much of his days were spent in therapy relieving us of the mentally exhausting task of having to fill dead space. It was heartbreaking to see our once dynamic friend in such a feeble, vulnerable condition.

Daytimes were especially hectic with numerous trips back and forth to see Jack and for every day we were there, Jenny looked forward to our evenings together. After a late dinner, sometimes home, sometimes at a local restaurant, we would sit up until the early hours of morning, reviewing the happy and not so happy events of our lives. More often than not, we took advantage of the spectacular southern California weather by sitting outside on Jenny's balcony under the millions of dazzling stars, accompanied by a bottle of bourbon or red wine, whatever we chose for the evening's pleasure. As worn out as Jenny may have been from the stress, tension, and fear of Jack's illness, she was still as beautiful as ever.

"I'll never forget the first day we met," she reminisced, "You guys were auditioning for a high school play as the Three Stooges!"

"Ah! To think that's how it all began," I fondly remembered, "I don't know if you knew this or not, but all three of us had the hots for you back then!"

"Oh, you had the hots for everyone back then," Willy snickered.

"Oh, let him flatter me," Jenny giggled.

Every night for three weeks, we toasted our long-lasting friendship and somehow never ran out of things to talk about. As we reminisced, we rejoiced over the good times and recalled how we toughed out the tragedies, knowing that everything we'd lived through was a lesson learned. As wonderful as it was to recall how rich and rewarding most of our lives had been, it was uncomfortably eerie to review the recent past and sense the inevitable end of the line.

One evening Jenny was mildly yet entertainingly buzzed and from out of the blue she turned to each of us and asked, "If I ask you a personal question, John Colletti and Willy Taylor, will you answer me straight?"

Willy and I gave each other a quick gaze of curious surprise and I answered, "We have no reason to lie or keep anything from you Jennifer!"

"Tell me then," she continued inquisitively, "Were either one of you guys unfaithful while you were on the road?"

Willy grinned and answered immediately, "Had plenty of opportunities, but never once did I succumb to temptation…"

"What about Marisa?" I probed, "You're not being honest, my friend. You definitely had something going on with Marisa Tomei!"

"I'm glad you think so," Willy said amused, "In my dreams, maybe!"

"What do you mean in your dreams?" I repeated unbelievingly, "She couldn't keep her hands off you."

"She was just a friendly flirt, my disappointed friend. Nothing more! I knew it was killing you guys." He held the piece of jewelry that dangled from his neck between his thumb and forefinger and said, "Tracy's dead, why would I lie?"

"Holy shit," I confessed, "All these years you certainly had me fooled!"

"What about you, John Colletti?" Jenny cut in like a gossip hound, "Any secrets you've been hiding?"

"Oh, he's been telling me his escapades since high school," Willy laughed, "Problem is, I never know when to believe him or not!"

"You were just jealous," I teased.

Jenny continued prodding, "Come on, John, give it up. It's not like I can rat you out to Joanna."

"Alright, alright, I'll submit," I said appeasing her, "There was just one time when we were in Arizona filming *Sedona*..." and I told her all about the night I spent with Julianne Moore's girlfriend. I hesitated here and there as I told the story and kept my eyes on the floor. I still felt the guilt.

After hearing my confession, Jenny took a sip of her bourbon on the rocks and nodded for a few moments before she spoke. "You know, John," she said pensively, "It's all right. The older I get, the more I realize that kind of shit's going to happen...Why the fuck not? It's just life...experience it, grab whatever the fuck you can before you end up like Jack." She paused for a few seconds, swirled the ice around in her glass, then continued, "Shit, it doesn't mean you didn't love Joanna...I may have done the same thing if I were you!"

Getting Jenny's approval didn't make me feel any better for having lied to Joanna. I knew she would have been devastated had she ever found out, not to mention that the life we knew would have been over. I sat quietly for a few moments, and then I asked Jenny, "How did you feel when you suspected Jack slept with some sultry actress in Hawaii? You wouldn't let him live it down, but nothing even happened!"

"I know," she admitted, "Double standards? I guess it's easier to accept when it's going on in someone else's life and not mine, but it doesn't mean I don't understand how and why it happens."

The conversation in those early hours of the morning had turned into a dissertation on regrets, deprivations, compromises, soul mates, and the moral implications of extramarital affairs. Nothing was solved, nothing was settled, but we certainly succeeded in venting and baring our souls. That was the last night of what had turned out to be a month-long stay. Jenny's two sons were due back in San Diego the following day when their dad was to be released from the rehabilitation center. It gave Willy and me peace of mind knowing Jenny would have their assistance in caring for Jack at home where his therapy treatments would continue. When we returned to West Palm, we remained in daily contact with Jenny until she convinced us that Jack was showing signs of improvement. We made a promise to visit at least twice a year, and on our second visit, although he appeared to have aged considerably, it delighted us to hear his speech was back to normal. We never brought up the subject of working again, assuming Jack must have realized The Three Extras were cinematic history.

As the years continued to fly by, Willy and I settled down and our trips to California and our communication with the Reilly's became less frequent. Our families were making regular visits to Florida, and Willy had even taken a stab at dating again. One afternoon, he invited Irene to come by. She was a nice looking widow who appeared to be in her early sixties; Willy never got the nerve to ask her how old she was!

The Three Extras

They met when she recognized Willy at the local Panera's as one of the Three Extras. It was a sterling day. The sky was blue and cloudless, the sun was in full splendor and it was a comfortable 82 degrees. Willy had asked me to join him for happy hour at his place so I could meet his new friend. As the three of us sat poolside sipping Willy's specialty, Gran Marnier margaritas, Willy asked if she minded if he remove his shirt. Irene had no problem at all with his request until she noticed the gold plated capsule dangling from the chain around his neck.

"That's a very unique piece of jewelry," she remarked, "Can I ask you what it is?"

"Sure," Willy replied matter-of-factly, holding the trinket on his fingertips, "I keep some of my wife Tracy's ashes in it!"

Irene's eyes bugged out of her skull as if Willy were some freakish ghoul. As she gagged on her drink, she trembled and said, "I'm sorry, but that's pretty fuckin' strange. I don't think you're quite yet ready to date so I'll show myself out!" and she hastily fled from Willy's yard. He looked at me, I looked at him and we shrugged our shoulders.

"Guess I won't be wearing this anymore," he laughed while removing the amulet from his neck. "Even in death she's warding off the women!"

John Rullo

~THE END OF THE LINE~

    I remembered what my father told me when he reached his 80th birthday. "Johnny," he wisely advised, "The older you get, the faster the time goes. Live your life to the fullest, because it's a quick ride!" The paperwork showed I had already lived eighty-four years though I couldn't believe it for a second. Sometimes I felt as if I had dreamt everything I knew to be my life and was going to wake up one morning a schoolboy. Time didn't seem real. The image in the mirror didn't resemble in the least who I felt was dwelling within me. If it was even possible, Willy and I grew closer every day. We'd been friends for over seventy years and had been through heaven and hell together. We knew each other's thoughts, anticipated each other's moves and loved each other deeper than brothers.
    It was April 29th, 2037, Jack's 85th birthday. The one thing we never failed to do was call each other for our birthdays. I spoke to Jack, who seemed to be in pretty good spirits. His three children and their families all flew out to be with him on his big day. Normally, Willy and I would make the effort to visit, but for some reason, neither one of us were up for it, figuring that we'd make the trip later in the year. Jack had been extremely talkative. I wished him a happy birthday and promised that Willy and I would be out to see him in a few months. Usually he would tell us how much he missed us and how he couldn't wait for our next visit. This time, however, our conversation took a strange turn. Jack had always been an optimistic sort of fellow. Although he knew to embrace each

moment, he mostly lived his life looking forward to the next project ahead; rarely did he mention the past. The entire dialogue consisted of Jack resurrecting moments of our long-ago past. He brought up Frank, the guitar player from our band. He rambled on about the high school plays, the college films. He recalled the time when Willy and I met Tracy and Joanna. He went on and on at great length as if he was reviewing all the highlights of his eighty-five years. I could hear Jenny in the background chiding him for being rude by staying on the phone so long and ignoring his children and grandchildren.

"Go enjoy your family, my friend," I said, taking advantage of the pause brought on by Jenny's interruption, "I'll talk to you again soon!"

I mentioned to Willy how strange I found my conversation with Jack to be. He didn't seem like himself. It didn't feel as if it were really Jack who was doing the talking. His dream-like retelling of past events was extremely out of character. Willy agreed by saying he shared the same experience when they spoke earlier in the day and how his keen intuition was alerting him to something not being right.

"We probably need to make a trip out there soon," I suggested.

"Yeah," Willy agreed, "Very soon!"

Three days later, on May 2nd, I got the chilling call from Jenny that my friend, partner and motivator had died in his sleep. As soon as I heard her voice, I knew. Emptiness came over me unlike anything I have ever felt in my life. Emotions swirled through my being, twisting my heart until the pain of the loss wouldn't allow me to hold back my tears any longer. I was sitting on the side of my bed, clutching the phone in one hand and staring at my image sobbing in the mirror. As devastated as I was when Joanna passed away suddenly, Jack's death affected me strangely different. Accepting his demise was like sensing the end of the journey for me. The swiftness of time and the absurdity of life overwhelmed me. Maybe Jack knew, and that's why his memory was running rampant during our last conversation. How many years, months, days remained before Willy and I became distant memories? How was I going to handle it should Willy check out before me? I had to pull myself together. I had promised Jenny I would pass along the news to Willy and rather than tell him over the phone, I dragged myself next door. One look at my bloodshot eyes and Willy knew.

"It's Jack?" he questioned as if he already knew the answer.

"Just got off the phone with Jenny...he died peacefully in his sleep."

"I had a premonition," Willy confessed sadly, "The last time we talked it was like he was saying goodbye...he fuckin' knew..."

"As good as life can be, my friend, sometimes it's really fucked up!"

I followed Willy to the den where he reached for the bottle of Makers Mark that was calling us from the bar. "On the rocks?" he asked.

"No, Willy, give it to me straight up."

Willy poured two healthy tumblers of the bourbon, we clicked our glasses and in unison we toasted, "To the Three Extras!"

The family had decided to fly Jack's body to his home town in New York where a wake would be held to celebrate his life with a traditional burial to follow. Willy and I may have missed his eighty-fifth birthday, but there was no way we were going to miss out on saying goodbye.

The Three Extras

~FAREWELL~

The sudden shrill cry of the morning alarm launched me into a sitting position. I was exceptionally groggy, feeling as though I had just fallen asleep only seconds ago. Did I actually view my entire life as it projected on the hotel room ceiling or did I simply dream it? It took several minutes for my confusion to settle. I finally grasped what I was doing in a hotel bed. It was difficult to accept that on this day I would be saying a final farewell as my friend's body got lowered into the cold brown earth. I shuddered at the very thought of it.

It was already seven thirty; a half hour had passed since the alarm startled me. We had to be at the church for nine o'clock so I reached for the phone and dialed Willy's room.

"You up?"

"Now I am," he replied, "Good thing you called, I fell back to sleep! You sleep alright?"

"I don't know," I answered a bit bewildered, "My mind was certainly working overtime last night, that's for sure…"

"Yeah," Willy empathized, "I had a rough time falling asleep myself…Thinking too much, I guess."

"I know what you mean. We better get moving," I advised, "I'm gonna jump in the shower, it's gonna be a long day."

"I'll be ready by eight thirty," Willy complied, "I'll knock on your door when I'm set to go."

The Three Extras

Jack and Jenny were never churchgoers, but for reasons I could never understand, continued to consider themselves Catholics. I couldn't remember the last time I stepped foot inside a Catholic Church, or any church for that matter, and gazing about at the statues of angels and saints and the morbid scenes on the stained glass windows, I was overwhelmed by uneasy, eerie and bizarre feelings. I couldn't imagine how in this day and age Catholicism hadn't long faded into oblivion.

Saint Jude's was filled almost to capacity. The Reillys had been a popular, well-liked and admired family long before Jack became a celebrity. Friends, neighbors, one time little-leaguers now adults, and folks we had known from the entertainment business all showed up to pay their respects and say farewell. Noticing Wendy sitting among the crowd raised emotions in me ranging from sadness to delight, causing my throat to tighten and my eyes to water. When our eyes met from across the rows she nodded and smiled. It had been years since I'd seen or spoken with her. We heard she had retired not long after Jack became ill, and retirement must have suited her well; she looked rested and amazingly healthy, a far cry from the frazzled, pushy go-getter I remembered.

Willy and I took our places in the pews just behind the immediate family. It was moving to see Jenny surrounded by her children, grandchildren, and their significant others. I remembered like it was yesterday the day when Jenny cried on my shoulder after finding out she was pregnant with Lorraine. Here was Lorraine, much older than we were then, sitting among beautiful children of her own. My thoughts were once again drifting back in time, spinning wildly when suddenly the sound of church bells tolling prompted everyone to rise to their feet as pall bearers slowly and solemnly carried Jack's coffin to meet the priest waiting at the front of the altar. Donned in white vestments, the priest circled the coffin gently swinging a gold incense burner as the smoke rose to the rafters and its sweet fragrance permeated the room. The sad sounds of sniffles and tears echoed above the meek voice of the celebrant as he spoke in a heavy accent, "Let us pray…"

    Willy and I followed the procession in our rented car to St. Rachel's cemetery. It was a mild spring day, mix of sun and clouds as we headed east for the thirty minute drive on the Long Island Expressway. All the years we've known Jack and Jenny, we never discussed the things associated with death such as cemetery plots, funeral parlors and wakes. We just assumed Jenny was going to have Jack's body cremated as we had with Tracy and Joanna, but obviously we had assumed wrong. Never did she once make any mention she and Jack had purchased plots in the event of their deaths.

    "Willy," I said breaking the silence, "When I finally go, my kids better honor my wishes and have me cremated. I don't want to ever put anybody through this ritualistic craziness."

    "Same here," Willy agreed, "Let's make a promise; if I go first, you see to it that I get my wishes and if you go first, I'll do the same."

    "It's a deal," I said, then thought for a second and asked, "What if we both go at the same time?"

    "Then it's their problem! What the fuck are we going to care? We'll be dead!" he cackled.

    The procession of cars for Jack's funeral was one of the longest I had ever seen. When we arrived at the cemetery, it took at least an hour for the attendants to direct all the vehicles into parking spots and all the participants to the gravesite. The funeral directors distributed red carnations as everyone huddled together to listen to the chaplain recite the words from his prayer book, "May perpetual light shine upon him and upon the souls of all the faithful departed through Christ our Lord, Amen. And now one by one would you kindly place your flowers upon the coffin, say your final goodbyes and find your way back to your vehicles. The family cordially invites everyone to join them in a luncheon in Jack's honor at Puccini's of Floral Park..."

As I placed my carnation on the pile of flowers, I whispered, "I'm going to miss you my friend, thanks for everything." As if it were scripted, at that very moment a cloud passed over, blocked the sunlight and made everything appear a dismal grey. Willy and I dragged our heels, slowly making our way to our car and for the entire drive to Puccini's were lost in our thoughts, neither of us uttering a word.

Jack would have loved the luncheon, seeing all his friends and family enjoying the very fine cuisine of his long-time favorite neighborhood restaurant.

"It's worth repeating," I said fondly quoting one of Jack's favorite lines, "You can always tell a good restaurant by the sauce!"

"Don't forget, 'an epidural is the way to go!'" Jenny laughed recalling his advice for the labor pains on the night of her first delivery.

Throughout the afternoon, several heartfelt toasts were made as stories, laughs, and tears were shared by all who loved him dearly. Willy and I had the opportunity to reconnect with Wendy who surprised us by attending. Thanks to her show biz eye and her keen intuition on the day we first entered her office, she was enjoying a well deserved retirement. The Three Extras and Wendy were deeply indebted to one another; neither of us could have achieved the level of success we did without the other. Wendy was beside herself when the news of Jack's passing reached her just two days ago. She put her life on hold just to attend his funeral. Wendy understood we had a fair amount of mingling to do. She gave us each a tight hug, thanked us for everything, gave us her new number and asked us to kindly stay in touch. The gathering lasted well into the early part of the evening when after some gentle prodding by the restaurant staff, the crowd began to disperse until all who were left were Jack's immediate family and us.

It was a long, stressful, emotionally draining day. Jenny pleaded with us to come back to Lorraine's house to unwind with a cocktail or two, but we were both talked out, worn out and weary. We had a morning flight back to Florida and after not getting any sleep the previous night I couldn't wait to hit the sack. Jenny walked us out while holding tightly onto each of our hands. Words weren't necessary; we knew how much we cared for one another. When the valet drove up with our car, the three of us embraced with every ounce of our strength. Jenny kissed us goodbye and as she wiped away the tears that involuntarily escaped from her grateful eyes, she called out, "I love you John Colletti...I love you Willy Taylor!" Willy drove back to the hotel and once again, neither one of us had much to say. The sun had set and the evening clouds had drifted in to obstruct the moon. Willy knew my thoughts as much as I knew his; there was no need to verbalize. We proceeded as if we had been programmed; zombies trudging along intent on devouring some sleep. Like two sleepwalkers, we traipsed through the lobby, into the elevator and along the 10th floor hallway until I stopped in front of Room 1012. Willy continued along to the next door and without looking my way mumbled clearly enough for me to understand, "I love you, Johnny boy."

I opened the door to my room, raised my voice to be certain he would hear me and replied, "I love you Willy Taylor." With my eyes at half mast, I got undressed, left my clothes on a pile on the floor, pulled down the blankets and dropped onto the bed where I slept uninterrupted until the sounding of the morning alarm.

    It was June of 2038; a little over a year had passed since Jack died. We made it a point to stay in touch with Jenny, who decided to sell the place in San Diego and move in with Lorraine. We were all in pretty good shape, health wise, for 86 year olds. Willy's prostate was a little enlarged but his doctor assured him there was nothing to worry about. I had no idea what may have been wrong with me because I refused to go to doctors. Maybe that's why I felt so good and lived so long. My motto has always been if it's not broken don't try to fix it. We were experiencing extremely hot weather in southern Florida and Willy and I were contemplating spending the summers in New York. I still had the house in Wantagh. For some reason I just never got around to selling it. Maybe I knew one day I'd be back! My sons looked after it for me, renting it from time to time, and from what they kept reporting, after a series of major hurricanes Long Island weather had begun to get nicer and nicer year after year in spite of the frightening predictions from meteorologists and oceanographers.

    Willy and I were sitting at my kitchen table having lunch one sweltering afternoon when the temperature reached 109 degrees. It was way too hot for the beach, even too uncomfortable for the pool.

    "What the hell's wrong with us," I questioned, "Why don't we just get the fuck out of here and go up north for a few months?"

    "Just need someone to push me I guess? Book us some flights, my friend, and we're there!"

I walked over to the fridge to add some ice to my drink when the phone rang displaying an old familiar New York number.

"Hello," I said curiously.

"Hello, Mr. John Colletti?" a young female voice replied, "John Colletti from the Three Extras?"

"Yes," I answered, "This is John."

"Hi John, my name is Brenda Mills and I'm the new proprietor of The Starlight Agency in New York City and I've heard so much about you fellows…"

"You have?" I interrupted, "I hope they were all good things?"

"Of course they were, John; can I call you John?"

"You can call me anything you want my dear. At this point in my life what does it even matter?"

Willy was curious as hell, motioning me from the table, whispering "Who's that; who's that?"

I waved my hand at Willy beckoning him to be quiet as I listened to what Brenda had to say.

"Okay John, I'll call you John. Well as it is, I think I may have an interesting role for you fellows…"

"Do you have any idea how old we are?" I cut in.

"Yes I do, John. That's precisely why I called you gentlemen," she said excitedly, "I've been requested to find three retired actors, preferably in their eighties, to play just what you are, retired actors!"

"Hasn't anyone at your agency been informed that one of the Three Extras has passed away?" I asked surprised.

"Oh no," she said apologetically, "I'm so very sorry. Was it recent?"

"A little over a year ago," I told her.

"Was it Mr. Taylor or Mr. Reilly?" she questioned.

Wondering why it would even matter to her, I answered, "It was Jack; Jack Reilly."

"Well, John," she resumed, "Would you and Mr. Taylor be interested in the roles?"

I paused for a moment.

"Mr. Colletti…John…are you still there?"

I cleared my throat. "Oh yes, Brenda, I'm still here…Thanks for the offer. Mr. Taylor and I are flattered you thought to ask us but we have to pass…"

Not willing to take "No" for an answer, Brenda persisted, "This could be a great opportunity for you fellows; HBO has…"

"Excuse me Brenda," I said cutting her off again, "Mr. Taylor and I are not interested. You see, it's always been the three of us, or none of us," and with those words I ended her call.

Willy stared at me with eyes full of questions, "What was that all about?"

I handed him the phone and said, "I'll tell you after you book us a flight to someplace cool. We need a vacation!"

~THE END~

Made in the USA
Charleston, SC
15 September 2013